THE WRONG MAN

THE WRONG MAN

George G. Gilman

NEW ENGLISH LIBRARY

For
Mick and Hazel
another couple
of dog nuts

A New English Library Original Publication, 1982

First NEL Paperback Edition November 1982

NEL Books are published by
New English Library,
Mill Road, Dunton Green,
Sevenoaks, Kent,
Editorial office: 47 Bedford Square, London WC1B 3DP

Printed in Great Britain by
Hunt Barnard, Aylesbury, Bucks.

British Library Cataloguing in Publication Data

Gilman, George G.
  The wrong man.
  Rn: Terry Harknett   I. Title
  823'.914[F]   PR6058.A686

ISBN 0-450-05517-5

CHAPTER ONE

THE man rode the black gelding out of the coastal strip of giant redwoods and paused briefly before he heeled his mount forward again. To move at the same easy pace across the soft sand of the broad beach toward the gently breaking surf at the edge of the ocean. He kept the horse headed slightly north of due west, so that he was able to gaze at the calm infinity of the Pacific directly in front of him without need to crack his eyes against the full glare of reflected light of the mid-afternoon sun.

The lone rider who crossed this driftwood featured stretch of deserted northern California beach was about forty. Perhaps a half inch over five and a half feet tall and built on lean lines – but there was an unmistakable stamp of strength on the way the man was put together. His face was unremarkable, the features regular in an arrangement that gave him a kind of nondescript handsomeness. His eyes were jet black, there was a suggestion of gentleness about his mouthline, and his hair – cut short but allowed to grow somewhat wild in sideburns – was mostly grey. And there were many deep furrows cut into the element burnished flesh of his face.

At first, second or even third glance, this is the impression a casual observer would receive of the man who rode across the thirty yard wide, slightly down sloped beach. Just this, plus the obvious fact that he was unshaven for many days.

He was dressed for western rough riding in a black Stetson, heavy duty boots without spurs and a sheepskin coat that concealed most of what else he wore – except for a grey kerchief at his throat. All his clothing was old and travel stained. And the gelding also had the look of an animal which had seen better days many weary miles away from this ocean shore.

And the horse snorted and quivered in equine relief when he was reined to a halt and his rider swung down from the saddle. This just short of where the blue ocean broke white along a strip of sodden, hard packed sand.

There was more than mere weariness in the way the man dismounted. And he arched his back, flexed his shoulder muscles and sighed his pleasure as he lowered himself gently down on to his haunches. Then became aware that the warmth of the sheepskin coat – so welcome in the deep shade of the giant redwoods – was not necessary out here in the bright glare of the hot sunshine. And while with the forefinger and thumb of his left hand he tried to work some of the tiredness out of his red rimmed dark eyes, with his right he began to unfasten the coat buttons.

He yawned, his mouth gaping open to its widest extent.

And this was how it remained during the full second he was able to experience the sensation of the bullet drilling into his flesh.

Then he clamped his mouth closed, his teeth crashing together so hard that it pained him. Hurt so much that he was no longer conscious of the bullet in his back.

He grimaced and heard the crack of the rifle shot

that had blasted the bullet at him. Saw the ocean get suddenly bluer, felt the heat become abruptly far more intense and heard the once peaceful thud of the breaking surf expand to an ear-splitting crash.

The bullet in his heart had stopped the organ's vital pumping function by then. And there was no time to indulge in melancholic regret that his life was to end this way. For as his brain was starved of fresh blood, the world of this man on the very brink of violent death was – for the final part of his last second of life – even more surreal.

Its colour was entirely white. Its sound was reduced to a rushing noise of variable pitch. Its taste was salt. Its feel was wet. It had no smell.

And he died without realising why all this was so – that the impact of the bullet had pitched him forward from his squat, to sprawl him face down in the breaking waves.

Where he was gently pushed and pulled by the action of the ocean at its edge.

Overhead, gulls screeched.

The gelding backed off a few paces and tossed his head.

The back shooter came out of the giant redwoods at the same point the rider had emerged. And advanced slowly along the tracks in the sand left by the horse.

He was dressed more suitably for the unshaded heat of the California afternoon – wore just a white cotton shirt without sleeves, buckskin pants that were pale green in colour and moccasins. No hat, but then he did have a head of thick, long growing black hair: long enough to almost brush over his shoulders with its ends and thus framed his entire face.

The face of a half Indian, half white. In his late forties or early fifties. The face long and lean, like the near six feet tall frame of the half breed. With angular features – the eyes sunken, the nose pointed, the cheeks hollow and the jaw jutted. The shape and set of the features entirely Indian. While the colour of his skin and the dark bristles that sprouted on the lower portion of his face revealed that he was not purebred.

He carried a Winchester rifle in two hands angled across the front of his shallowly rising and falling chest, the muzzle aimed at the cloudless sky to his left.

For three fourths of the way from the fringe of the trees to where the corpse was gently moved by the ocean's tideline, the half breed advanced like an automaton. Then, some twenty or so feet from the dead man, he halted his measured strides. And wrenched his unblinking stare away from the half floating, spreadeagled form in the surf. To glance down at the rifle.

His face expressed a silent snarl. And he pumped the lever action of the rifle. To eject the expended shell of the fired bullet and jack a fresh one into the breech.

Then he aimed the Winchester at the bobbing form in the white water and completed his cautious approach. Halted again with his moccasined feet just inches away from the tideline: and the snarling set of his features changed to a grin of satisfaction when he saw the neat hole – cleaned of blood by seawater – in the coat of the face down man. Precisely far enough left of centre for the bullet to penetrate the man's heart.

The gulls continued to screech in shrill and raucous counterpoint to the regular dull thud of the breaking surf.

For the first time since he showed himself at the fringe of the timber, the half breed looked elsewhere but at his victim and the rifle.

Gazed north to where a rocky point jutted into the ocean some three miles away. Then shaded his eyes and squinted to survey the coastline southwards where, about five miles distant, a wooded rise with a black cliff base ended the beach in this direction. Just variegated pieces of misshapen driftwood featured the broad swathe of fine yellow sand.

To the west, no ship was close enough in shore to be seen.

And in the east, back of the slight slope of the beach, there was just the great forest of massive giant redwoods. Teeming with life, but all of it as invisible to the half breed as that which inhabited the ocean.

The half breed's rifle was unaimed while he surveyed the beach in both directions, and the ocean. While he raked his no longer smiling eyes over the timber, though, the muzzle of the Winchester tracked along the same vista. Then, still tense – and casting a constant stream of suspicious glances toward the cover of the nearest section of forest – the killer turned his attention to the horse of the dead man. Held the rifle in just his left hand now, as his right became busy with the fastening of one of the saddlebags.

The black gelding submitted without protest to what was happening: content to stand idly in the warmth of the sun after being ridden so many miles through the chill of the forest floor. The impulse to fear triggered by the rifle shot and its effect long since gone.

The bag's fastening came free and the half breed delved a hand under the flap. Explored the interior blindly for a few moments, then made to look into the bag.

But sensed danger.

Snatched his hand from out of the bag. To fist it around the barrel of the Winchester. Next powered into a whirl and a half crouch.

A series of sudden moves that created fresh fear in the brain of the gelding. Caused the animal to turn away from the half breed and lunge along the hard packed strip of beach: hooves tossing up clods of sodden sand.

The half breed was like a granite statue for a stretched second. Then wrenched his head to the side to stare down at the buoyantly moving corpse. Jerked it back up and around again: to gaze at the man who had ridden his chestnut mare out of the giant redwoods.

Depthless terror was abruptly carved into every plane and hollow of the half breed's face. This as his eyelids were stretched open to their widest extent. And his mouth gaped to vent a scream of horror – that took perhaps two full seconds to find voice. For this length of time was as if petrified again.

Then he swung half around, away from the stranger who had reined in his mare when the Winchester was aimed at him. Began to run, which was easy for the first few strides. But then the hard packed sand was behind him and the fine, dry grains gave way under his pumping feet so that he had to drag free each trailing leg before he could throw it forward to become the leading one.

He stared fixedly ahead again now – but more fearfully than when he came so much slower down the beach. He no longer screamed. Instead trailed behind him in the saline air an eerie, almost animalistic wailing sound. Which set the seagulls to screeching again. And threatened to drive the horse of the dead man into a fully fledged bolt.

But then this sound, too, was curtailed. For the half breed needed to suck air into his lungs. After which he could only pant – the terror that triggered his dash for the timber far more draining than the exertion of ploughing through the clinging sand.

Then he was on firm ground, racing through the trees: beads of sweat spraying away from his face in his slipstream. He had angled across the beach, heading north east, in an effort to constantly widen the gap between himself and the stranger who was approaching from the south east: and also to gain the cover of the timber in the shortest possible time.

He knew when he was in cover – had to veer to left and right to get around the trunks of the towering trees. But his terror was undiminished and he ran faster still – as fast as the firm ground and his reserve of energy would allow. Never once looked back to see if he was being pursued. Eventually pitched into a forward sprawl of physical exhaustion. And lay face down on the carpet of rotting redwood detritus. Panting and weeping and trembling. The mouth in his fear contorted face working to form words which had no sounds. In English and the Apache language, as he prayed to God and to the Great Spirits. Begging forgiveness for the wrong he had committed in killing the man, and imploring that he be immune from the evil that had been unleashed by the murder.

By which time, the man who had aroused such a degree of dread in the half breed was at the very edge of the ocean: having ridden slowly, a hand on the stock of his booted rifle, after the running man went from sight. Rode with his cautious attention divided between what was obviously a dead body floating at the tideline, and the fringe of the timber.

Then, after sitting his halted horse for perhaps fifteen seconds – while the black gelding tentatively approached the chestnut mare – he decided that the frightened half breed was not about to make a rapid recovery from hysteria and return. And he dismounted, dropped down on to his haunches and reached for a booted foot of the corpse. Caught hold of it at the first attempt when a breaking wave floated the body closer. Then quickly straightened and stepped backwards. Managed to keep his boots out of the water as he dragged the whole length of the dead man clear of the ocean. Then stooped and, with one hand on the shoulder and the other on the hip, flipped the corpse over on to its back.

Grimaced as he muttered: 'Can see why that feller reckoned he'd seen a ghost.'

A man named Ethan Winston, now sprawled out on his back on the wet sand, might well have been the identical twin brother of the one who gazed down at him. A man named Adam Steele.

CHAPTER TWO

STEELE perhaps weighed a few pounds more than the dead man. And he had shaved this morning. Also, among his prematurely grey hairs were a few that still gave a clue to the auburn that he once had been.

Apart from these minor differences, all else about the two men appeared to be identical. As identical as the knee length sheepskin coats which they wore.

Not so the rest of their clothing. For Steele's Stetson was grey and although his unspurred boots were black, they were more stylishly made than those of Winston. And beneath the topcoat which he now removed, he wore a grey, city style suit, a yellow vest and a white shirt with a black bootlace tie knotted at the throat. A grey scarf of silken fabric hung loosely around his neck — this, like the snug fitting buckskin black gloves on his hands, much older than the rest of his outfit.

Not normally the kind of man to show his feelings, Adam Steele displayed obvious surprise for many stretched seconds as he continued to stare down at the face of the dead man while he took off the coat. And still felt uncomfortably warm — not entirely from being out in the direct glare of the sun.

Then a man shouted.

'Hey, mister!'

Horses snorted and hooves beat on the sand.

'That there a breed you plugged?' a second man demanded to know.

Steele tore his gaze away from the unnerving sight at his feet when the first shouted word reached him. Then had swung around and taken a step toward his mare before he saw the two riders. Had the sheepskin coat flung across his saddle and a fist around the frame of the booted rifle when the question was yelled.

The skittish horse of the dead man sidled away from the sudden activity. But did not bolt.

Adam Steele, the mare between himself and the riders, rested a gloved thumb on the hammer and curled a forefinger to the trigger of the Colt Hartford, but did not slide the rifle out of the boot.

The riders came down the line of tracks left by Ethan Winston's gelding and the half breed. The gallop quickly giving way to a weary walk as the soft sand dragged at the hooves of the horses. And the eager excitement of the men in the saddles was drained by the sight of Steele with a hand on the rifle.

'Shit, we don't mean you no harm, mister!' the one on the piebald gelding assured. He was about fifty, tall and with a muscular build that was starting to run to fat. Blue eyed and black bearded.

'Jesus, Vic!' the other man — riding a grey gelding — rasped as he hauled his mount to a halt. 'It's Ethan all dressed up like he was gonna go on the town with a woman and —'

'No it ain't, Ryan!' Vic gasped, and halted his horse ten feet closer to the edge of the ocean. Stared at the corpse and then pointed a finger at it as he completed: 'There's Ethan, all drowned!'

14

Ryan was a few years older than Vic. A head shorter and a great deal lighter in weight. He had an emaciated, gnarled face with black eyes that shone like polished coal — and widened as they flicked from the face of Steele to that of the dead man and back again.

Both Vic and Ryan were dressed in baggy pants and check shirts, with kerchiefs knotted at the rear. They wore battered and stained Stetsons and scuffed work boots. Each had a gunbelt slung around his waist, with a Colt Peacemaker in a loose hanging holster on the right. Vic had a single shot Springfield rifle jutting from a boot on his saddle.

Men and mounts were weary and ill cared for at the end of a long trip. In many respects were a match for Ethan Winston and his horse. But in the matter of facial features and physical build, nowhere near as alike as the dead man and Adam Steele.

'Ethan didn't drown, feller,' the dudishly dressed man with a hand on his rifle explained, his accent so pronounced that he might have left the Virginia of his roots only a few days ago.

'Uh?'

Ryan had moved his horse up alongside that of Vic, seeking to ease his anxiety by being close to his partner. Neither of them made a move toward drawing a gun. Both continued to be as fascinated as Steele and the half breed had been by the striking similarity between two men.

'He was shot in the back, feller. By a half breed Indian. Maybe the one you thought he was?'

Steele gestured with his head toward the corpse.

'Damnit, I ain't never seen nothin' like this before,' Ryan muttered, still flicking his eyes back and forth between Steele and the corpse.

15

While Vic had to make a conscious effort to avoid looking at the corpse, and he gazed fixedly at the Virginian to say:

'Ethan never told nobody he had no twin brother. But then he never was much of a talker. This here is Ryan King and I'm Vic Judd. And I guess you're kinda anxious to know why what happened to your brother did happen, right Winston?'

He climbed wearily down from his saddle as he spoke and gestured with a movement of his head that King should do likewise.

'Name's Adam Steele, feller,' the Virginian answered. And released his grip on the booted rifle. 'Which makes none of this any of my business.'

He loosened the ties fixing his bedroll to the saddle, so that he could push the sheepskin coat under them.

'Steele?' King posed.

'Not Winston?' Judd asked.

'Right both times,' the Virginian answered, but failed to convince the two men. Who stood beside their horses, reins in their hands.

'Ethan sure wasn't from the south, Vic,' King said to Judd. 'Like this gent sounds he is.'

'From Keysville, Virginia,' Steele supplied. 'Kind of family that wouldn't have had any skeletons like an unwanted twin in the closet.'

'Ain't it said that everyone's got a double somewhere in the world, Vic?'

'I've heard that,' Steele answered as Judd's incredulity came close to being suspicion. 'And it was sheer coincidence that me and mine happened by this stretch of the coast at the same time.'

'You mind sayin' just why you happened by here, Mr . . . ?' Judd asked.

'Steele, feller. If your business isn't mine, I reckon —'

'Good reason for askin',' the bigger built, younger and more untrusting of the two said quickly.

'None that I care about, feller,' Steele countered and, for the first time, there was a degree of coldness in his expression and his tone of voice that struck a chord of fear within the two men. Which transcended Judd's distrust and King's continued fascination with the likeness between the Virginian and Ethan Winston.

After Steele had shared the icy look between the two of them, he nodded his satisfaction with the resultant effect and swung up into his saddle. Apparently nonchalant again, but not shifting his gaze away from the men.

Vic Judd seemed to be seeking a form of words to capture Steele's interest. And Ryan King spoke first.

'There's some dust been stole, Mr Steele!' he blurted. 'And Ethan's partner was killed! Dan Webb! The breed done it and me and Vic and some of the other guys —'

'Don't want you to grab hold of the wrong end of the stick, mister!' Judd cut in, with a withering glare at King. 'Ain't Ryan nor me makin' any accusations of you!'

'No offence taken, feller.'

'We're from Golden Hill,' Judd hurried on when Steele made to heel his horse forward. 'Small place up in the hills back of the redwood forests. Where folks dig for gold and sometimes strike lucky.'

'Not very lucky, you understand, Mr Steele,' King put in. 'Ain't nobody ever got rich at Golden Hill.'

'Ryan?'

17

'Yeah, Vic?'

'Just needs one of us to tell it.'

King looked contrite, then embarrassed and finally peeved. But he just shrugged his skinny shoulders. While Judd grunted and returned his intent gaze to the impassive face of the mounted man.

'Well, mister, to get to the point, there was some trouble at Golden Hill a few nights ago. Trouble of the worst kind.'

'Four nights,' King put in and vented a grunt of satisfaction of his own.

'Yeah. Dan Webb and Ethan Winston, they got themselves a joint claim. And are maybe the best two buddies at Golden Hill.'

'Better'n us for sure!'

Judd ignored this interruption, too. 'Anyways, four nights ago, Dan gets his throat cut open, ear to ear. While the poor slob is sick with fever and alone at the claim. And Ethan is at the cathouse of Miss Sophie. But, lucky enough, Ethan is through with the whore and headin' for home in time to see the breed takin' off from the claim like he was tryin' to outrun time. The breed, he's just kinda like a nigger at Miss Sophie's place. Does all the shit work only a nigger or a Chinaman or a breed would do, you understand?'

'Breed didn't kill old Dan for the hell of it, Mr Steele.'

'I'm gettin' to that, Ryan,' Judd snapped, and moderated his tone. 'I'm gettin' to that, mister. Dan, he had a store of dust. Worth close to a thousand dollars, Ethan figured. Well, that dust was missin' after Dan was found dead and the breed had took off.

'Ain't no law at Golden Hill, but all of us there

18

knows right from wrong. And there's some of us willin' to right a wrong when one happens. And so a bunch of us got together to make up a vigilante troop and we come after the breed. But he's more Injun than he's white and he covered his tracks real well. So us vigilantes — eleven of us there was — we split up to try to pick up the sign the breed left.'

Ryan King opened his mouth to interrupt again, and Vic Judd glared at him. Adam Steele said evenly:

'The half breed went that way.' He raised a gloved hand to point along the line of the tracks left in the sand by the fleeing man. 'Running faster than ever he did before, I reckon. Way I see it, terrified of me because he thought I was Winston come back to haunt him.'

King nodded several times. 'I can see how he'd think that, Mr Steele. You give me and Vic a start, that's for sure. The breed bein' mostly Injun, he'd be real spooked and no mistake.'

'The breed just up and shot Ethan?' Judd asked.

'That thousand dollarsworth of dust is the reason for all this, feller?'

King gulped. 'Like Vic said, Mr Steele, ain't nobody accusin' nobody of nothin'.'

'I didn't see the shooting,' the Virginian supplied. 'Heard the shot.'

'Like Vic and me did and —'

'Shut up, Ryan,' King snapped, without shifting his nervous gaze away from the face of the mounted man.

Steele signalled with a head gesture toward the sprawled corpse whose clothes were drying fast in the warmth of the sun. 'When I came out of the

19

trees, he was dead and floating in the ocean. And the half breed was at the horse.' Now he nodded toward the black gelding. 'I was halfway from the trees to here when he turned and saw me. And took off. That way, like I already told you.'

'Breed must have spotted Ethan on his trail, hung back and let him pass, Vic!' King said excitedly. 'Then crept up on him and backshot him. Get rid of him and steal his horse. Only this gent spooks him. The breed, he took off on foot from Golden Hill, Mr Steele. Never did have a horse of his own there. And didn't have the time to steal one when Ethan spotted him —'

'We're much obliged for you helpin' us, mister,' Judd cut in, after looking long and hard at the dead man's black gelding while his partner was talking. 'Certainly would seem that it happened the way Ryan says. Figure we oughta bury Ethan here and get after the breed real fast.'

'You held me up, feller. Not the other way around.'

'I ain't sayin' different, mister. I don't know.' He scratched in his beard and shrugged his shoulders. 'You lookin' so much like Ethan. And bein' right here with the corpse. With the breed gone. Hell, with all the dust and all . . . '

'That's better, feller,' Steele said, and the chill was back in his tone of voice and the way his dark eyes glistened. 'Stop talking before you say enough to give me offence. Good day to you.'

He heeled the mare forward, riding between the black gelding and where the two men stood beside their mounts, to head back up the beach along the tracks he made coming down it. Then reined the mare to a halt just a second or so after the men and horses were behind him — when Vic Judd commanded:

'Hold it, mister!'

'What the frig, Vic?' Ryan King said, shocked yet again, as Steele looked back over his shoulder. To see the bigger man with the beard scowling at him — and aiming the Peacemaker. While King stared in horror at the man.

'Shut up, and go check the saddlebag on Winston's horse!' Judd growled. 'The one that's open.'

'Check it, Vic?'

'Look inside it, for frig sake!'

'What for?'

'Jesus!'

'Okay, okay! But why'd you have to draw against this gent?'

He trudged through the sand, taking care not to cross between the steadily aimed revolver and the Virginian. While Steele and Judd continued to keep their gazes locked together. The mounted man impassive. The one with the gun becoming increasingly more disconcerted by the total lack of reaction.

'Hurry it up, will you!'

'Okay, okay!'

Steele sat his saddle, with just his head turned, in an attitude of surface calm: feet resting easy in the stirrups and gloved hands fisted around the reins just above the horn. But beneath this apparent patient indifference, he was tensely poised to react immediately to the first hint that Judd intended to trigger a shot at him.

'Shit, Vic, it's here!' King yelled in shrill high excitement. 'In that same buckskin poke old Dan always toted it around in!'

21

Just for part of a second Judd looked to be undecided. And for that same brief span of time Steele remained at the peak of readiness — tensed to hurl himself off the horse, sliding the rifle from the boot as he went. Counting upon Judd missing him or only winging him with the first shot. Certain that if this happened, he would be able to make sure the big, bearded man did not have time to fire a second.

But then the man jerked the revolver down to his side, eased the hammer gently forward and found some relief for his own tension in a short, gruff laugh.

'Proves it happened just like Ryan said, don't it?' he said huskily as he slid the Peacemaker back in the holster. 'The breed just had the time to put the gold in the bag before you showed up to spook him?' He wrenched his gaze away from the trap of Steele's — to snatch a glance at his now equally afraid partner before he looked back at the mounted man again. Asked: 'What d'you think, mister?'

'What I'm trying not to think of, feller, is what would have happened if he hadn't found the gold in that saddlebag.'

'Jesus, mister, I'd have had Ryan search you, is all. Just to be sure that you hadn't —'

'Vic and me's gold grubbers, Mr Steele!' King pleaded. 'We pack guns for our own protection is all.'

'Anyway, no harm done to any of us!' Judd blurted with a bright grin that was heavily strained. 'You can go about your business, mister. Ryan and me, we got the gold dust to give to Dan Webb's next of kin. And we can get Ethan Winston buried and get after the breed again. Bring him in for two killin's now. No hard feelin's, uh?'

'Reckon not, under the circumstances, feller.'

Some of the strain went away from Judd's grin. And King's tension was released in a draught of cooling air he blew up over his sweat beaded face. But then both men were suddenly apprehensive again. This as Steele pursed his lips, like he was about to vent a low whistle. Instead, directed a globule of saliva over his shoulder and the rump of the mare to the sand.

Judd's grin became a scowl without any effort as he snarled: 'I been spat at before, mister. It don't bother folks like me when dudes like you —'

'Vic!' his partner warned.

'Just commenting on the circumstances, feller,' Steele said evenly. 'It shook me up a little, too. Seeing my dead spitting image.'

CHAPTER THREE

VIC Judd laughed harshly and Ryan King rasped more warning words at him – the less intelligent man failing to grasp the point of the black humour and worried that his partner might be ridiculing the unresponsive Virginian.

But then the bearded man explained the joke and King exploded a burst of laughter. More forced than that of Judd had been.

Steele was almost at the edge of the timber by then, far enough away for the itch to be eased between his shoulder blades. For he was out of effective range of either man's Peacemaker. And knew from the directions from which their voices reached up the beach to him that neither moved toward a rifle – the Springfield of Judd or the Winchester in the boot slung from the saddle of Winston's gelding.

Then he rode into the cover of the redwood forest and was mildly surprised to feel the extent of the chill as the sweat dried on his face and some areas of his body – had not been aware of just how much he was sweating out in the unshaded sun.

But the heat of the California afternoon had little to do with the way his pores had opened. Likewise the aiming of the revolver at him by Judd and the possibility that this man or his partner might shoot him in the back as he rode off the beach. All three were doubtless contributory factors. But the main cause of the hot sweat turned suddenly cold now was certainly the unnerving experience of hauling the corpse out of the ocean, turning it over and gazing down into the face of a man who looked so much like himself.

An experience which, despite his efforts to remain untouched by it – at least in terms of his outward responses – had dictated his attitude during the interlude with Judd and King. Two men who were maybe still alive quite simply because of the profound effect the shock of seeing Winston had on Adam Steele.

He did not become unsettled easily, this eastern dude who was forbidden to return to his home state. Perhaps the last time he had been so badly shaken was immediately in the wake of the crime which destined him for the life he now led. A life so vastly different to the one he lived before the War Between the States.

Back then he had enjoyed the luxury and privilege of being the only son – the only child – of Benjamin P. Steele, perhaps the wealthiest plantation owner in the entire state of Virginia. But during the war, the elder Steele elected to support the Federal Government against the Confederate cause. A loyalty that aroused vicious spite in the immediate aftermath of the war's end – the plantation and its big house were put to the torch by unknown southerners soured by defeat.

This at about the same time as another group of fanatics were engaged in the assassination of President Abraham Lincoln. A political murder in which Ben Steele, an innocent bystander, became tragically involved.

26

Adam Steele had served the Rebel cause as a cavalry lieutenant – as bitterly resentful toward his father as he was toward every Yankee while the Civil War raged. But when peace came, he was ready and willing to accept his father's invitation to a reconciliation. And went to Washington in good spirits.

There had to cut down the corpse of Ben Steele from the beam in the bar-room where he had been lynched. There, too, committed his first killing in a peace that was destined to be as violent as war had been. Next rode home, unaware until he got there that it no longer existed. But was able to bury his father on the Steele estate. And was given, by his best friend of pre-war days, the only item of value saved from the fire in the big house – a Colt Hartford sporting model rifle. A six-shot percussion rifle of .44 calibre. With a revolving action. Its rosewood stock scorched, but the inscribed gold plate screwed to it not touched by the fire. The inscription reading: *To Benjamin P. Steele, with gratitude – Abraham Lincoln*.

It was with this rifle, which rode in the boot now as he moved through the giant redwood forest of northern California, that Adam Steele avenged the lynching of his father. Trailing the killers across the eastern states, and was in turn trailed by the law. One representative of which was Deputy Jim Bishop, the old friend who ensured the rifle passed from father to son.

Bish felt duty bound to take Adam Steele back to face trial – for acts which in time of war were not illegal. Felt, too, that in the circumstances justice would be tempered with mercy. But the ex-soldier was not prepared to submit to such a courtroom test. And the only way to avoid this was to kill his old friend Bish.

He could recall precious little of events on the long trail from Tennessee – where he murdered Jim Bishop – to the Mexican village of Neuvo Rio. Where, in the cantina, he was in a drunken stupor for almost a month. After which he forswore liquor: both because he had lost the taste for it, and because its effects proved to be only a palliative and not a cure for what ailed him.

Just once since then had he taken a drink – a single shot of whiskey because of the loss of a woman. But what he discovered about Lucy was, he decided now, not so shocking to him as the killing of Bish and the sight of a dead man who was his double.

For, back on the sun bright beach a few minutes ago, it was as if Adam Steele were dead – had come full circle from the vicious killing of the deputy sheriff to his own violent end. Was precisely what the half breed had superstitiously assumed him to be – a disembodied spirit come to look upon the shell from which death had separated it.

Since he emerged from the long drunk in Neuvo Rio, the Virginian had ridden countless miles along hundreds of western trails. For most of the time aimlessly and for much of the time in danger of getting killed. Often surviving only by killing those who sought to kill him. Living from day to day and never getting to keep for long anything that was worthwhile. Accepting the fact that such a drifting existence, with the possibility of lethal danger lurking at every bend in the trail, was a more severe form of punishment than any man-made justice could have meted out to him. At first.

Then, after he learned to want nothing that was

not readily available, he abandoned such a self-pitying philosophy. Became as utterly cold and lacking in compassion as he was forced to be in the war and while he was tracking the killers of his father.

So long as he could eat, sleep and protect himself from the elements, he was content. If the opportunity to dress well presented itself, he could sleep between silken sheets or had the money in the right place to dine in a first class restaurant, so much the better. Likewise with friendship, be it with men or with women. If he felt the need when something was offered, he accepted. But he paid his way, in cash or kind. And when it was taken from him, he shed no tears as he turned his back on what once had been to head for what was to come.

And what was to come, inevitably, was death. A death which, because of the kind of life he led, would surely be violent.

On a day when he could not get the Colt Hartford clear of the boot and to the aim fast enough, or failed to hit a vital spot with the throwing knife he carried in a boot sheath. Fumbled an attempted strangulation with the thuggee scarf that was draped around his neck. Perhaps would have no opportunity to even try to retaliate. Be bushwhacked from behind the way Ethan Winston had been. By a new enemy or one of many made in the long and blood spattered past.

For what?

Somebody else's trouble and a few dollars he was paid to take a hand in it. A few dollars needed to keep himself and his horse from starving.

The Virginian shivered, not entirely from the

sweat striking cold on his flesh. But reined in the mare so that he could put on the sheepskin coat. Heeled the animal forward again – towards what and where?

He did not know and, perhaps worse, he did not care. Beyond that certain knowledge of ultimate, inevitable death.

And that was the damn trouble: the reason he was going hot and cold since he saw a palpable image of the way he would look if today he was to be violently killed. Sprawled face down in the sea . . . or the sand . . . or amid the needles and cones carpeting this forest floor. Alone and unmourned, which did not cause him any regret. But having achieved nothing worthwhile was a distressing notion. As, also, was the thought that – if he died today – it would not be while he was in pursuit of any laudable end. Or any damn end at all – short of the basic ambition of staying alive.

For today was like so many others since he killed Bish and thus destined himself to be unlike almost every man he had ever met. There had been a range war of sorts over in Wyoming and he had taken a hand in that and survived to ride the open trail toward the next explosion of trouble. Which had taken many days extending into weeks to announce itself – as a distant rifle shot sounding through the redwood forest.

Not that an isolated rifle shot in game country such as this had to mean trouble. Which was one reason why Adam Steele did not urge the mare to greater speed when he altered course to head in the direction from which the shot sounded. Another reason was that he was not sure if he was ready to make human contact again.

And, the way it turned out, it had been a mistake. Trouble it was. Not of his making and with nobody who was involved wishing him to take a hand in it. The entire episode a waste of time and nervous energy. Which left him feeling drained and depressed. And angry at himself for being so.

But this mood did not last for long. He had always been a fatalist, but was also a realist. The accident of coincidence happened all the time and he and Ethan Winston had been as likely to come face to face when both were alive as they were when one was dead.

So it was not an omen.

And there were hundreds of occasions when Adam Steele had been closer to death than he was today. Occasions during and after which it would have been much more appropriate to reflect upon the emptiness of his life.

He was alive still. Which he had to consider made him a whole lot better off than his double. And, he also had to allow, he much preferred to be himself than anybody else he had ever met. And what more could any man ask than to be alive and to envy no other?

A voice pleaded: 'Help me.'

From in front of the Virginian and over to the right, beyond a thicket of thorny brush.

'Please. I'm drownin'. Hurry.'

A man who sounded very weak. And now, after Steele had halted the mare, began to sob as he wailed:

'Please don't torment me any more! If I have to die here, let it be soon and in peace! Don't cheat me into thinkin' help's comin'!'

Then the tone of the man's voice altered as he began to speak in a foreign tongue. Which, after he

31

heard a few words, the Virginian was able to identify as the language of the Apache Indian. Identify it, but not understand it. Though guessed the half breed on the other side of the thicket was now asking the Great Spirits much the same as he asked the Christian God.

The brush grew thick to a height of some twenty feet between the massive trunks of two towering trees. And Steele had to heel the mare into movement and turn her to back track some hundred feet to go around one of the redwoods before he could see the half breed. Who continued to wail his pleas from out of a private world of religious fervour to which the sights and sounds of a terrifying reality were barred.

Steele said nothing, but took no pains to cover the sounds of his approach. Which he halted about seventy-five feet short of the man who was in danger of drowning. But not in water. Was sunk to his armpits in a patch of mud coloured quicksand: slowly but inexorably being sucked deeper.

'Hey, feller!' the Virginian called sharply as he swung out of the saddle. And drew the Colt Hartford from the boot, to hold it in one gloved hand – fisted around the muzzle end of the barrel.

It was evening now on the floor of the forest. But probably at the brightest time of the day, it would be difficult to see where the solid ground gave way to the treacherous surface of the quicksand. Especially so for a man who was certain he was fleeing from a ghost. And who was now convinced that ghost had found him.

'No!' he screamed. 'Please, let me die in peace! Leave me alone, Ethan Winston!'

His head had been tilted back so that he could peer up through the treetops. And his arms were raised, palms turned and fingers clawed as if he were trying to take a grip on some ethereal being who was reaching down to pluck him from the quicksand. But at the sound of Steele's voice he snapped his head and arms down and around. To stare at the Virginian and thrust out his arms, hands now held in an attitude of rejection.

'I look like him, that's all,' Steele said. And started forward, slightly stooped so that he could prod at the ground ahead with the stock of the rifle.

'No, don't come near me!' the half breed implored, terror driving his voice to a shrill pitch.

'If I don't get closer, feller,' the Virginian answered evenly, 'you're going to be stuck with that sinking feeling.'

CHAPTER FOUR

THE man in the quicksand was still capable of rational thinking to some degree. And while he continued to be in dread of what he was convinced was the departed spirit of Ethan Winston, he also realized that in struggling to get away from it he was speeding the downward slide of his trapped body.

And he forced himself to remain utterly still. The expression on his exhausted face and the attitude of his outstretched hands still designed to repel the Virginian who drew nearer a cautious half step at a time.

'I killed you because you would have killed me, Ethan Winston.'

'Don't reckon you have any idea where the firm ground gives out and the sand starts?' Steele asked.

'You are not there! I will ask that your ghost is taken from my sight!'

Now he tilted his head back again and raised his arms. Looking toward and reaching for the sky. Praying intently but with quiet words. In the Apache tongue.

It was apparent he had ran full tilt into the area of quicksand. Still terrified by the episode on the beach. So probably did not even know he had turned to come south after he started out running north. Blundered through the forest until he realised something other than exhaustion was slowing his pace. Was forced to a halt and looked down at where his feet and lower legs were being sucked into the sand. He would have begun to struggle then, as this new menace took priority over the old. Managed to half turn around – seeking to get out the way he came into the patch – before he was made to realize there was no hope of dragging himself free.

Then, no longer struggling, he had been gradually dragged deeper – his sole hope that before he was entirely submerged his feet would touch solid ground.

Maybe he had prayed.

Or perhaps he had been prepared to accept his fate – as punishment for killing Ethan Winston. Even welcomed death, by whatever means, as preferable to a life of being haunted by the dead man's ghost.

It was getting darker by the moment and Steele was having a hard time concentrating on the task he had set himself. The ground beneath his feet and under the prodding rifle stock was made springy by the accumulation of leafmould from the thicket of brush. And he was conscious of a difficult to control urge to panic. A sensation totally alien to him.

'Hey, breed!' he snarled, and stopped his advance, still thirty feet from where the head and upstretched arms of the man were just visible through the gloom. But the prayer to the Great Spirits of the Apache faith was not curtailed. And the Virginian roared this time: 'I'm talking to you, you crazy sonofabitch!'

The silence in the wake of the monotone entreaty was a great relief. And Steele, for the second time that day, realised only when it turned cold on his flesh that he had been sweating heavily.

'That's fine, feller,' he said, his voice much lower

now. 'Pray if you have to, but I'd appreciate it if you'd do it quietly. Also like for you to reach out a hand toward me. So I'll know when I can stop heading out into –'

'You don't talk the same as when you was alive, Ethan Winston.' The half breed still sounded afraid, but there was an underlying tone of awed resignation in his voice. His pale face showed as a dirty white blur against the backdrop of evening shadows.

'I don't?' Steele answered and went forward again, behind the exploratory rifle.

'You deserved to die, after you killed Mr Webb. You have to admit that.'

'Yeah.'

'And for tellin' everyone at Golden Hill that it was me who done it.'

'I told them that?'

The period of disturbing disorientation was gone now and Adam Steele felt totally in control of his emotions again. Knew the half breed could see him as just a shadow against shadows and that this was helping him to conquer his fear of the supernatural. And it was a deliberate course to go along with the idea that he was the ghost of Ethan Winston. Since this also contributed to the calmer mood of the man.

The stock of the Colt Hartford snapped a dead twig and sank an inch into the clinging grip of the edge of the quicksand.

'You know you did, Winston!' the half breed countered as Steele jerked the rifle clear and dropped to his haunches.

'It all seems a long time ago. I don't remember too well.'

He set the rifle down, to mark the point where the

patch of dangerous ground began. Fifteen feet from the half breed who, if he extended an arm, could reduce the distance by more than two feet.

'You was at Miss Sophie's place. Had some beer and went with the new girl. Emily. Don't you remember that?'

'No, I don't remember that, feller.'

Steele straightened up, after delving a hand through a slit in the outside seam of his right pants leg. To bring the knife out of the boot sheath.

'Don't leave me!' the half breed implored as the Virginian turned to go back the way he had come.

There was an impulse to anger now. Toward a total stranger who had at first begged for help, then been intent upon spurning it and now wanted it again. By a man who had felt by turns strangely not himself, moved to panic and then disconcertingly doubtful of why he was doing what he was doing – all of this happening to somebody who hardly ever needed to consciously think about being in control of his emotional responses.

He came to an abrupt halt now, and directed a fixed gaze back over his shoulder. Spoke in a tone that was bitingly hard.

'Look, feller! We've both had a rough day. Maybe you had a rougher one than me. But I don't care much about you. I'm not Ethan Winston. I just happen to look a lot like him. My name's Adam Steele and it's of no interest to me what Winston did to his partner and you. Nor what you did to him. Going to do my best to get you out of there because I think you want out. Like you said at the start. Before you saw me again and spooked yourself.'

'I sure want to –'

'Shut up and listen, feller!' Steele cut in on him, so viciously it caused the man to gasp. 'I reckon I got spooked back on the beach when I looked at a dead man who might have been me. But I was getting over that real well just before you got my attention again. And I had some more crazy thoughts for awhile.

'But they're finished with. And pretty soon you'll be finished with, far as I'm concerned. Either sunk in over your head where you are. Or out here getting over it. In either event, I'll be going about my own business. You understand, feller?'

'Yeah. Yeah, I guess so. It was just that when you started away, I figured you'd given up on me. All that stuff before . . . gee, I want out of here, that's for . . . but –'

He couldn't find the words to express his feelings and so decided abruptly to give up the search. Steele, also, said nothing as he located and cut a twelve foot length of strong and reasonably straight brushwood. Then trimmed off all but two of the side branches – these the two thickest at the thickest end of the pole. Next went to the mare and cut a rigging tie off the saddle – used this to fix the unbarbed end of the pole to the reins.

Now asked: 'You still in the land of the living, feller?'

'I guess so. But I'm going down all the time.' He sounded relieved and scared at one and the same time.

Steele held the pole in his right hand and led the horse by the bridle with his left to go toward the quicksand again. Able to see just various shades of black on black. So he slid each foot forward, until at length the toe of his boot touched the rifle – and he had to apply conscious force to bring the sole and

39

heel up from the clinging ground. Discovered when he crouched down that the Colt Hartford had settled slightly into the edge of the quicksand.

'Your arms still out?' Steele asked after he had returned the rifle to the boot.

'Yeah.'

'Cover your head, feller. Going to toss a pole out to you and I don't want to brain you with it.'

'Okay, I'm all covered up.'

The Virginian gritted his teeth and firmed his hold on the bridle. Then tossed the pole into the darkness with the action of a lance throw. Quickly transferred his free hand to the nose of the mare. And was stroking her and murmuring soft words of reassurance when the pole hit the sand with a moist sounding thud. The reins were jerked taut.

The animal tossed her head in response to the unexpected tug. But could only half complete the movement, which was wrenched to a halt. The half breed yelled:

'I got it!' Then vented a cry of pain. Complained: 'Shit, that almost took my arm outta its socket!'

'Just hold on!' Steele countered in a rasping tone through his still gritted teeth. Then softened his tone as he returned to calming the horse while he continued to stroke her.

'You can bet I will.'

Now the Virginian, actions and tone of voice still gentle, urged the mare to back away from the edge of the quicksand. Stroked her neck as he tugged on the bridle and murmured:

'Atta girl, back up. Easy, easy, easy. Come on, you can do it.'

For long seconds the grip of the quicksand

remained solid on the form of the half breed. And the man clinging to the end of the pole snarled:

'Move it, you bastard! Put your friggin' back into it!' Then he cried in pain again. Next vented a burst of laughter before he blurted: 'Hey, it's workin'! I'm movin'! Damnit, that nag is doin' it!'

At first the mare moved just her head. To overcome the initial inertia. Then became disconcertingly aware that her forehooves were sinking into the softness of the ground where leafmould layered on firm earth gave way to the unstable sand. Which triggered an urge to fear in her equine brain. And she may well have struggled to turn and then to bolt had not Adam Steele continued to calm her with a gentle hand and reassuring words. So that she kept going backwards, in the unnatural gait that demanded the pace be slow.

Slow but constant. So that, once it was moving, the weight and bulk of the half breed's form was dragged inevitably toward the edge of the patch of quicksand. Then out of it.

Unable to see what was happening to the man he was rescuing, and too intent upon controlling the mare to be aware of the ground he was covering, Steele could not be sure of what caused the reins to go slack.

'Easy,' he murmured to the horse, as he tugged on the bridle to halt the animal. Stroked her nose again and asked of the half breed: 'You out of it?'

A sound that was part sob and part laugh was vented by the man. Who then managed to blurt:

'I ain't never been happier to be anywhere but where I am.'

'Fine,' the Virginian said. And stooped to draw the knife again as he hauled in the reins. Cut the tie and re-sheathed the knife. Swung up astride the saddle and told the man who he could now hear taking great gulps of air into his lungs: 'I'd hate for the horse and me to have gone to all this trouble for nothing.

'Uh?'

'Best you get out of this part of the country fast. Couple of fellers named Judd and King are looking for you around here. And they said there are some more people from Golden Hill who mean to find you and –'

'I didn't do what Ethan Winston told them I did, mister. I didn't kill Dan Webb and I didn't steal his gold . . .'

Steele had wheeled the mare and her hooves thudded into the sound deadening leafmould as he rode the horse back toward the point where he could get to the other side of the wall of brush between the trees.

' . . . Hey, where you goin'?' the half breed wailed after he had broken off to listen to the horse – for long enough to discern that his rescuer was leaving.

'Like I told you, feller. About my business. And you said you understood.'

'Yeah, but that was before! You saved my life and I wanna pay you back.'

'Only want the one thing right now,' Steele called as he rounded the massive trunk of the giant redwood and resumed the path he was following when the half breed called for help.

'Right now, mister, I'm right out of every damn thing except for gratitude. But you say what you want, and if it ain't impossible to get, I'll get it for you!'

'The quiet life.'

'Shit, I –'

'And to give me that, all you have to do is keep your word until I'm out of earshot, feller. In your mouth.'

CHAPTER FIVE

THERE was no moon to filter its light down through the dense growing foliage of the towering redwoods. So in this near pitch darkness and with the memory of the patch of quicksand fresh in his mind, Adam Steele allowed the mare to make her own pace. Relying on her sharper animal instincts for natural dangers to assure safety. While he was able to dictate the direction of the ride – southward, with the distant thud of surf against the shore constantly off to the right. Which was easy enough and allowed him to concentrate on remaining alert for the first hint that a man triggered menace was about to be unleashed at him.

A state of readiness behind an easygoing nonchalance that he was able to maintain without any tendency to be falsely alarmed by the sounds and movements of forest creatures or the occasional wafting of an ocean breeze among the trees.

Which was a state of affairs he relished at the ending of this day during which, twice, he had been unnerved by experiencing feelings that were out of character and therefore were unpredictable.

Now, though, as the forest began to thin at its southern end and he was able to see a little further in the light of night that was less shadowed by more widely spaced redwoods, he felt entirely in control of his emotional responses. This as he sought a suitable campsite for a night that was going to be rain soaked, located such a spot and swung smoothly out of the saddle. Bedded down the hobbled mare, built and lit a cooking fire and set some coffee to boiling and some pork and beans to cooking. By turns whistling tunelessly but contentedly and grinning foolishly as he went about these chores on an area of sand under a slightly jutting wall of rock behind the broad beach of a small inlet.

The rain held off while he cooked and ate the food. And the wind from the north, which gusted and then became constant, caused him no problems because the thirty feet high and twice as broad wall of rock sheltered the night camp. It was noisy, that was all: howling and moaning and crackling among the trees, and piling, rushing and driving high surf at the beach.

Then the rain came, and sizzled out the already dying fire. Proved to be an ally of the Virginian as he sat wrapped in his blankets, drinking a second cup of coffee. For the norther had started to pick up grains of sand and send them in minor whirlwinds across the base of the bluff. And some of these eddied at him. But the rain, which at one moment was no more than dampness on the wind and the next was a torrential downpour, turned the surface of the beach into a sodden mire too heavy for the wind to disturb.

Steele drank the coffee and left the cup out in the rain to be washed. While he stretched out full length in his blankets, his head resting on his saddle and his hat covering his face. His gloved left hand fisted around the frame of the Colt Hartford that shared the warmth of the blankets – a thumbing of the hammer away from readiness to meet whatever threat a man or men of evil intent chose to direct at him. While his mind was cleared of all superfluous thought processes as he sank into a dreamless sleep: from which he knew he would awake with instant and total recall. And be ready to react to whatever was demanded by the circumstances of his awakening.

His uncluttered mind immediately able to command that he kill somebody. Or that he smile or scowl to greet whatever kind of new day had dawned.

He slept, that area between crystal clear awareness of his surroundings and the subconscious state of shallow but restful slumber having reduced the harsh and violent sounds of the California rainstorm to a muted level that was almost hypnotic.

And then he awoke. Sunlight was getting in under the brim of the hat covering his face. Likewise the gentle and regular sound of the unviolent surf thudding on the beach. And the smell of the ocean mixed with the fragrance of a redwood forest after rain.

A sense of being watched was less intrusive than any of this. But was more demanding of investigation. And so it was with this prime objective that Adam Steele withdrew a hand from under his blankets, raised the hat off his face and turned his head on the saddle pillow. While his other hand took a firmer grip on the rifle, thumb on the hammer and forefinger between guard and trigger. In a series of overt and secret moves that were unhurried and composed: for in sensing the presence of somebody close to him, the Virginian did not register any sign of aggression.

'Mornin', Mr Steele,' the man greeted.

'Breed,' the Virginian countered and folded up into a sitting posture, releasing his hold on the rifle to pick up his hat and put it on.

'My name's Joseph Mitchell. It's only folks who're bigoted against me call me the breed, Mr Steele.'

He was sitting on the largest of many chunks of rock which a long ago fall had scattered in the sand some thirty feet to the left of where Steele now rose to his feet, stretching and yawning, rasping the back of a gloved hand over the bristles on his jaw and blinking in the brightness of the light of sunrise reflected off the blue smoothness of the Pacific.

'You been there long, Joseph Mitchell?'

He had obviously slept, for his long and lean face did not have the haggard look nor his dark eyes the red rims of exhaustion. The teeming rain or a voluntary cleaning up had removed from his clothing all signs of his ordeal in the quicksand. They were wrinkled and stained by old dampness. But he was barefoot – perhaps had lost his moccasins when he was dragged out of the clinging ground. The rifle, too.

Although he was on the high side of fifty and there was in the structure of his face and the light in his eyes a stamp of innate intelligence there was, paradoxically, something almost childlike in the way he gazed at Adam Steele this morning. Never letting his curiosity filled eyes drift away for a moment from the Virginian who began to build another fire, to the side of the damp ashes of the first.

'I wasn't never more than fifty yards behind you when you was ridin' to here last night, Mr Steele.' He gestured with his head to indicate the top of the

48

bluff. 'And slept under a bank in some brush up there after you'd had your supper and bedded down yourself. Had a swim in the ocean just before sunrise. Been here an hour maybe. I'll be glad to take care of the fire and breakfast if you want.'

'Used to doing it myself, feller.'

The fire was built with brushwood he had gathered last night and stowed in the dry at the base of the outward sloping rock face. Now he struck a match on the cooking pot and lit the kindling.

'That's okay, Mr Steele. Whatever you want and say. I kept real quiet like you said you wanted last night, didn't I?'

'You move more like an Apache than a white man, feller,' Steele said as he delved into a saddle-bag. 'You want some breakfast?'

'I had some already, Mr Steele. Indian style, off the table nature provides. Live like a white for most of the time. Have done since my white Pa took me away from the Apaches after my Ma was killed. Was thirteen years old then and I'd only known the Apache ways before that. Pa liked them ways, too. Lot of what I learned way back when I was a kid I just never did forget.'

The Virginian put no food in the pot. Just water for shaving. He put some grounds in the coffee pot, though.

'Want you to know somethin', Mr Steele,' Mitchell said after a long pause, during which the Virginian had rolled up his blankets, booted the rifle and taken off his sheepskin coat.

'What's that?'

'Don't know if it's the white man in me or the Indian. But I mean to repay you for savin' my life.'

49

Still he kept close scrutiny over Adam Steele: and sometimes the curiosity showing in his dark eyes leaned close to incredulity. Making it obvious that he continued to be fascinated by the likeness between this stranger and the dead Ethan Winston.

'I can understand that, feller,' the Virginian told him. 'I'd feel the same if things had worked out the other way around.'

Mitchell grinned, displaying discoloured and crooked teeth. Asked: 'So you'll let me do that?'

'You have something in mind?'

'I don't have no money. On me or back at Miss Sophie's in Golden Hill, Mr Steele. So I can't pay cash. I worked at the house for just board and lodgin'. And I never was much for savin' cash or buyin' anythin' to keep at the places I worked before Miss Sophie's.'

'Wouldn't know how much to charge for a life anyway, Joseph,' Steele told him.

And he smiled again. A plaintive expression this time, as he stood up and said: 'Gee, thanks Mr Steele.'

'For what?'

'Callin' me Joseph like you did. It's what my Pa and Ma always called me. And the rest of the Indians down to the south. To whites I'm mostly the breed or somethin' insultin'. Sometime I get called Joe. But Joseph, that's really somethin' to me.'

The Virginian ignored him and tested the temperature of the water in the cooking pot. Decided it was hot enough for shaving and scooped out a cupful. Sat on his saddle and took a razor and cake of soap from a saddlebag. Began to shave by touch, with nothing reflective to look into.

'You know what I mean, Mr Steele?' Mitchell urged.

'I reckon so. Though it seems to me it isn't so much what a man's called as what he is that's important.'

'There ain't no denyin' that, that's for sure. But when a man gets called all sorts of names just because of who his parents were, that can get to stick in his craw.'

Joseph Mitchell had begun to pace up and down along the base of the bluff: between the rock on which he had been sitting and the fire on which the coffee pot was giving off an appetising aroma. And he was no longer gazing at the Virginian all the time. Talked in a rather vague way and wore a preoccupied expression – like he was projecting his thoughts ahead of the present subject and finding it difficult to frame what next had to be said.

Steele again made no response and finished the shave in silence. Dumped the soapy and bristle polluted water into the sand and asked of Mitchell:

'You want to borrow the razor, Joseph?'

The man interrupted his pacing and shook his head. Smiled briefly as he seized upon the opening the Virginian had provided.

'No thanks, Mr Steele. Reckon I'll grow me a beard. Could be cut my hair. And try to gain some weight. Change my name for sure.' He looked hard at the freshly shaved man again, but this time not in wonderment. Instead, inviting a question.

'Get said what you have to,' Steele supplied as he went to the fire. Where he rinsed the cup, filled it with coffee and returned to his seat on the saddle. 'My cup and my coffee, so you're second in line.'

Mitchell nodded. Then hurried on, like he was impatient after the short wait for Steele to get settled again.

'It's the God's honest truth what I told you last night. I didn't kill Webb and I didn't steal his gold. I started to tell you about it, didn't I. When I figured you for the spirit of Ethan Winston. Not only useful teachin's of the Indians stayed with me, Mr Steele. Some of the other stuff, as well. I really did figure you was –'

'I know it, feller,' the Virginian cut in reflectively. 'And it's nothing you should be ashamed of. I was taught that superstition was all nonsense. But yesterday was strange.'

'I ain't ashamed, not really,' Mitchell went on eagerly the moment Steele was through. 'Kinda glad I acted crazy in a way. Makes you more likely to believe me. When I was countin' on meetin' my maker any minute and figured I was talkin' to the spirit of the man I'd killed a couple of hours before. I wouldn't start tellin' no lies then, you figure?'

'Reckon not, Joseph,' Steele allowed.

'Like to finish tellin' what I started, Mr Steele. Important you should know all about it. If I'm to repay you the only way I can see how.'

Steele finished the coffee and handed the cup to Mitchell as he stood up. Then he saddled the chestnut mare while the half breed toyed with the empty cup and told his story.

'I have worked at the house of Miss Sophie for more than a year now. It is menial work, but not hard. And for most of the time I am treated well by the people of Golden Hill. I guess this is because for most of the time they treat me like I do not exist. In many other towns in many other parts of the country, things were very different.

'But that does not matter. Five nights ago was very different at Golden Hill. My work for the day is over and I am in my small room at Miss Sophie's house. Readin', because this is what I do most of the nights after my work is finished.

'There is a new girl in the room next to mine. Her name is Emily and she does not like me because I am half Apache. Ethan Winston, he goes with her and I overhear everythin'. Not from listenin' on purpose, though. In a place like Miss Sophie's, the walls are not thick and nobody cares usually.'

The saddle was now cinched to the mare and the Virginian hefted his bedroll on behind it.

'It is never of any interest to me, what goes on between the girls and the men. Always I go on with my readin' and pay no attention. But this time, Mr Steele, it's different. It wasn't so much what they was sayin' that caught my ear at first. More that they weren't doin' what usually happens in the rooms at Miss Sophie's. And how they was whisperin', guilty like.'

'You want any coffee, Joseph?' the Virginian asked flatly, his interjection and manner suggesting indifference to what was being said. 'Ready to douse the fire.'

Mitchell thrust the empty cup toward Steele with a gesture that told of anger. But he kept his tone steady and his expression neutral as he answered:

'No thanks. All I want from you, Mr Steele is a hearin'.'

'You're getting it,' came the even-voiced reply before the final chores of breaking night camp were undertaken.

53

'Okay, so I'll get to the point. It seems that Ethan Winston was real struck on this Emily. And she didn't like what she'd found at Miss Sophie's. They was plannin' on leavin' together. Goin' to San Francisco. But neither of them had any money which they'd need in the city.

'So they planned to rob Dan Webb of the poke of dust everyone in town knew he had. And it's what they done, Mr Steele. Killed him while they were doin' the robbery. Guess maybe they figured to trick him and take the gold and he cottoned on. I ain't got no way of knowin'. All I do know is that after Ethan Winston and the girl left Miss Sophie's place, I went on readin'. Which maybe a man like you finds hard to take, Mr Steele. But it's what I done. Until I heard all the hollerin' and the shoutin' and figured out what was happenin'. That Dan Webb was dead and robbed and I was gonna get the blame for it.

'Man like me at a place like that, Mr Steele. Was either stay there and get lynched for somethin' I didn't do. Or run. So I run for my life. Knowin' that it made me look guilty.'

Adam Steele had all his gear on the mare and the fire was out. He stood beside the horse, a gloved hand on the saddlehorn, listening to Joseph Mitchell in the same impassive and apparently indifferent attitude as from the start. He responded to the half breed's enquiring look now, though.

Said: 'I believe what you've told me, feller. And I can see why you had to leave town fast. You still haven't got to the point of all this, far as I can see.'

He swung up astride the mare and the barefoot man on the ground blurted:

'It ain't all told yet! What about me killin' Ethan

Winston the way I did, Mr Steele? I could easy lie to you about that.'

The Virginian pursed his lips and shifted into a more comfortable posture in the saddle. Gazed out across the broad beach to the sun sparkling water of the inlet for a few seconds. Then moved his attention back to the expectant half breed.

'Reckon that was cold blooded murder for gain, Joseph. From what I saw.'

The man on the ground stared intently up at the mounted one for awhile: like he was tacitly responding to what he considered to be a disguised challenge. But the Virginian's tone had been matter-of-fact and his element burnished and experience lined face was dead pan. So Mitchell suddenly looked away and adopted an attitude of shame as he hung his head. Was child-like again.

'It was that for sure, Mr Steele and I wasn't gonna lie about it. But you gotta see it from where I was. That bastard Winston and the whore had got a whole town after my neck for somethin' they done. They'd lost me the best place I'd ever stayed since my Pa took me away from the Apaches. At first when I started to run, I was just plain scared and only wanted to get away. But then I took some time to think, Mr Steele. Like a white and like an Indian. And after I'd done the thinkin', I took the action. It was real easy for me to throw them Golden Hill men off my tracks. The Apache teachin' again. Easy to circle round behind a pair of them and take a Winchester off one of them while they was sleepin'.'

The display of shame was short lived. Now, Joseph Mitchell was getting close to boasting as he spoke with lips which hardly moved from the line of a smile of pleasure.

'And then I went after Ethan Winston. Knew I was gonna kill him. Knew as well that he would have the gold he stole from Webb. And I was gonna steal it from him. I had to have it to give me a new start in life.'

Once again the expression on the pale face with its Indian bone structure underwent a radical change. From the prideful smile to a frown of malcontent – as he gazed out to sea and concluded bitterly:

'But you showed up, Mr Steele. And the whole lousy world blew up in my face again.'

'I've been there, Joseph,' the Virginian told the half breed. 'Maybe as many times as you. Maybe even more. Never helped me much to talk to somebody about it, but if you're feeling better –'

'I don't want no pity, mister!' Mitchell snapped. And shook his head violently as he transferred his anger at Steele to himself. 'Shit, I'm really messin' this up, ain't I? Look, I told you it all now and I'd like to hear that you believe it.'

'Told you I do, Joseph.'

The half breed pursed his lips and vented a low, short whistle of relief. Then:

'I'm real glad that's so, Mr Steele. Because the way I figure it, we're meant to stick with each other. And partners can't get along if they don't trust each other. And unless you believed me about –'

'Joseph,' Steele put in quietly but firmly.

'Yes, Mr Steele?'

'Way I am, two isn't company. It's a crowd.'

'You don't want me taggin' along with you, uh Mr Steele?'

'Right, feller.'

'Because you like to be on your own?'

'You got it.'

The Virginian tugged gently on the reins and touched his unspurred heels to the flanks of the mare. To head her slowly along the base of the bluff, intending to ride around the small bay that was at the southern end of the redwood forest and to the north of a strip of rocky terrain between the ocean and a range of grassy hills.

Joseph Mitchell shuffled his bare feet in the sand and turned to watch Steele's departure. Sad eyed and with hunched shoulders, his hands thrust deep into his pockets. Once more childlike in expression and stance. And there was a whining tone in his voice when he called after the man astride the horse:

'You ain't bein' fair, you know that, Mr Steele! You ain't allowin' me the chance to pay you back for what you done for me!'

The Virginian turned in the saddle as the mare continued to plod through the sand, going around the scattered rocks from the ancient fall. But looked at the disconsolate half breed over a distance of forty feet for just a moment. Before his attention was captured by two other men.

Who had ridden their horses around the seaward side of the bluff and reined them in. Some fifty feet in back of where Joseph Mitchell stood – his self pitying attitude abruptly frozen as he saw Adam Steele become tense.

The two newcomers showed as no more than dark silhouettes against the dazzlingly bright backdrop of the sunlit ocean. But from their size and shape and the way they sat their mounts, the Virginian immediately identified them as Vic Judd and Ryan King.

The half breed became anxious, snapped his head around. Saw the two men from Golden Hill and was once more in the grip of terror.

Screamed: 'No! I ain't goin' back to be lynched!'

His head came around again, to show his fear contorted features to the Virginian. And then he lunged forward. To race across this beach in much the same way he had covered the stretch of sand the previous day. Trailing a shrill vocal sound of fear in his wake. But on this occasion it was not away from Adam Steele that he ran. Instead, came straight toward him.

The bearded Vic Judd slid the Springfield rifle from its boot. The skinny Ryan King clawed the revolver from the holster.

Steele fisted his gloved right hand around the frame of the booted Colt Hartford. Thumbed back the hammer as he pulled the rifle clear.

The half breed came to an abrupt halt, ten feet short of where the Virginian threw the stock of the rifle to his shoulder.

'Oh, God no!' he groaned. And was like misery personified again – as he dropped his arms to his sides and his chin to his chest.

The Springfield rifle cracked out its shot. And the bullet went over the head of Mitchell. Came closer to drilling into the half turned upper body of Steele.

King began to trigger shots with his Colt as Judd hurled the rifle to the sand and reached for his revolver – also thudded in his heels to set his mount lunging forward.

'He created you, Joseph,' Steele rasped softly. 'Seems I'm charged with riding herd on his handiwork.'

CHAPTER SIX

THE emaciated Ryan King fired three shots from his Colt. In a panic, over a range of at least sixty feet. And his gun pulled to the left and down, so that all three bullets burrowed into the sand far short of his targets.

He was not able to fire again.

For his less impetuous partner was between the muzzle of his gun and the targets. Judd yelling at him that he was every kind of fool for wasting time and shells.

Judd's handgun was clear of the holster by then. Held out at arm's length over the head of the galloping horse. But unfired while he snarled the foul mouthed rebukes at King and waited to be sure of a killing shot.

Perhaps as enraged at himself as at his partner – for not taking the time to take more careful aim with the Springfield. This high emotion countered by the beginnings of another, less powerful one. Of quiet confidence that the city suited man half turned in the saddle on the chestnut mare was not a killer. That he carried the fancy revolving action rifle for the same reason he dressed in the fancy outfit.

For show was all.

Vic Judd's face even began to lose its look of anger so that the lines of a smile could start to form. This as he rode close enough to the Virginian to recognise the expression of indecision on the freshly shaved face.

But then Adam Steele completed his rasping comment. And as the half breed wrenched up his head to stare at him, he triggered a first shot from the Colt Hartford.

Saw Joseph Mitchell grin.

Saw the neat hole the bullet opened in the cheek of Judd – between the bristles of his beard and his left eye. One of a pair of eyes that was glazed by death before they had a chance to see a change come over the Virginian's features. So that the man with the rifle was again emanating the aura of the cold hearted, totally unmerciful killer he had hinted he was when Judd and King saw him on that other beach.

The range over which the rifle bullet cracked was about twenty feet. So that it had sufficient velocity to tunnel entirely through the head and explode out of the back. Amid a gush of blood. This as the dead man, still rigid from the shock of dying, was sent toppling out of the saddle by the impact of the bullet. Falling to the left – to crash among the scattered chunks of rock half buried in the sand – as the gelding veered to the right. The horse without a rider needing to act of his own volition to evade running down Joseph Mitchell and crashing into the Virginian's mare.

By this time the hammer of the Colt Hartford had been thumbed back again. And the rifle had been raked slightly to the left. So that the muzzle and the equally dangerous looking dark eye behind the backsight were aligned with the face of Ryan King.

A thin, gnarled face that wore an expression of

pathetic helplessness: as the man sat his unmoving horse in much the same attitude as when he had blasted the three panicked shots at Adam Steele. Now, though, he had brought up his other hand so that both were clasped to the butt of his revolver. Not thrusting it out at arms' length. Instead, with the insides of both wrists braced to his chest. But despite this, he could not keep the Colt steady. For he was trembling from head to toe after seeing his partner crash down among the rocks, trailing blood.

The Virginian saw the look on King's face clearly for just part of a second – when a shaft of early morning sunlight stabbed through the treetops on the rim of the bluff's eastern arc so he was no longer a dark silhouette against the ocean.

Then he shot the man. The Colt Hartford a rock steady extension of hands, arms and shoulders that at the instant of firing might have been as inanimate as the metal and rosewood of the rifle's construction. Except for the almost imperceptible movement of the trigger finger.

Another head shot, but his this time placed a little higher and more central – to drill into the skull and brain through the brow just above the bridge of the nose.

Because Ryan King was sitting a stationary mount and the bullet cracked across a longer range, this man's topple to the beach was less frenetic than that of Vic Judd had been. He bent backwards in the saddle, his lifeless hands opening to release the revolver that became wedged for a moment between his crotch and the horn. Then his slight weight shifted to one side and his opposite booted foot slipped from the stirrup. He slid down and across the side of the horse and his head sank softly into the sand. The gelding was unsettled at having the man doing what was virtually an ungainly headstand against him and side-stepped away. And the corpse fell with a thud to be full length on the beach.

'That's twice over I'm in your debt, Mr Steele,' the half breed said in a husky tone of awe as he shifted his eyes away from the now inert form of King to look again at the Virginian. No sign of a grin on his bristled face: instead he expressed the familiar child-like wonderment in his still scowling benefactor.

But the Virginian shook his head as his face became impassive while he thrust the deadly Colt Hartford back in the boot. Said:

'No, feller. Way it looked set to be at first. But when the shooting started, it was my skin I was aiming to save.' He raised a gloved hand to point to where Judd's gelding had halted on the far side of the inlet, then brought it back to touch the brim of his hat. 'Reckon that's the horse that's carrying the stolen gold dust, Joseph. Why don't you go get it and forget everything that's happened since you shot Winston? Luck to you.'

Once more he heeled the chestnut mare along the beach away from the half breed. And could sense the man's dark eyes gazing fixedly after him. But felt no impulse to look back. And Mitchell did not call after him.

Beyond the end of the bluff, Steele veered his mount off the beach and up a long slope of grey rock. Although the grade was not steep, it was featured with many jagged fissures. And he needed to devote his entire attention to traversing the dangerous ground. So it was only when he was at the crest of the high ground that it was safe to look down at the arc of beach in the small bay.

Saw that the scene below had not yet changed: that the riderless horses, Joseph Mitchell and, of course, the dead men and their discarded guns had not moved. And did not move now.

All that did was the quietly restless ocean as it lapped at the shore. The constant and relentless measured thud and run-off of the surf on the sand as persistent as the doubt that gnawed at Adam Steele's mind. But, unlike the shore, the Virginian was capable of physically drawing back from the palpable cause of his indecision. Which he now did. By turning his back on the scene below and riding inland to put distance and obstacles between himself and the half breed.

But, of course, a man cannot get away from the thoughts in his own head. And then, before the morning was more than an hour older, he knew he had something of greater substance than nagging self doubt with which to deal. For he realized he was being trailed by a lone rider.

A rider who was about a mile distant when Steele first saw him, halted on a ridge when he paused to decide which route to take along a valley. And, give or take a few yards, this gap between the trailed and the trailer never varied on the several other occasions when the Virginian saw the half breed. Such visual contacts made at random when the terrain was such that no rises intervened between the two men to conceal one from the other.

Initially, Steele was irritated by the presence of Mitchell on his back trail. For he thought only in terms of the half breed's nuisance value in keeping fresh the self doubt which, had he gone his own way, might have dulled and died. But then, during a pause for a midday drink of water and meal of cold jerked beef, the Virginian elected to examine the situation from a different viewpoint.

And discovered he felt as relaxed and in as good shape as when he bedded down at the night camp on the beach.

The place where he had called a halt to indulge in the midday break was at a point where the California terrain changed yet again. Several miles in from the coast, where the ocean could not be seen, heard or even smelled. On the fringe of the area of near barren rock hills and at the threshold of a much vaster tract of pastureland that for the most part rolled and only occasionally reared. Cut with count-less creeks and liberally scattered with small stands of mixed timber. Good growing and grazing land, but this section not yet settled. Somewhere to the south there were surely sodbusters and ranchers working other sections of the well watered and warm sunlit land. And maybe to the east, as well, on the lower slopes of the Coast Range of mountains.

But in the immediate vicinity there was just the half breed and himself. Mitchell still the usual mile away, but no longer north of where Steele was halted on the bank of a small creek at the side of a clump of sitka spruce. Instead, he had arced around toward the east, so that like the chestnut mare, his newly acquired gelding could drink from a stream and crop at some lush grass. The man and his horse on slightly higher ground and in clear sight of Adam Steele. The half breed who stood – not eating nor drinking – at the unshaded side of a stream, never shifting his gaze away from the Virginian. While Steele merely glanced toward the other man from time to time as he thought his way around to the new viewpoint.

Beyond this, neither man ever by the slightest gesture acknowledged the presence of the other one. Like they were not so much looking at, but through, each other. And it was this notion which triggered the process that led Steele to adopt another attitude toward Mitchell.

If the half breed wanted to act like his shadow, then that was the way the Virginian would treat him. And to think of him in terms of a shadow was to draw a fine parallel. A better one, even, than if it was Ethan Winston out there on his trail. For although that man had borne a truly remarkable resemblance to Adam Steele it had only been on the shallow surface. A simple physical likeness. Much more the Virginian's double in a deeper context was Joseph Mitchell.

Both of them – Steele and the half breed – two men inside the shell of one.

One a rich eastern dude who doubted he would ever fully adapt to the life of a Western drifter. The other torn between being an Indian and a white man.

Both of them capable of cold blooded killing, but only for a justifiable motive.

Joseph Mitchell desperately anxious to establish himself as an honest man despite whatever else he might be. Adam Steele a man who cared nothing of what others thought about him, but constantly strove to ensure they had no cause to doubt his integrity.

Had needed, too, on many occasions, to struggle against the temptation to indulge in bouts of self pity when the whole damn world and his brother seemed bent on making life hell. Just as the half breed had fought against such self indulgence this morning – in a manner that indicated he had a great deal of experience in this direction.

There were probably many other parallels he could draw between Mitchell and himself, Adam Steele reflected as he filled his canteens with the fresh, cool, sweet water of the creek. But he already had enough to serve his purpose – and to delve too deeply might invite a comparison with those aspects of himself and the other man which were disparate.

He hung the canteens on his saddle and then swung up astride it. Knew, without needing to look across the mile wide stretch of slightly rising pastureland that Joseph Mitchell was also preparing to ride again. Was conscious through the long, hot afternoon that the half breed was always behind him just as he had been during the morning. But now the Virginian no longer paid the slightest heed to him, whether he was in view or not.

In the same negative frame of mind toward the man as he was toward his actual shadow.

He had saved the life of Joseph Mitchell. Once deliberately and the second time incidentally. But, since he could not help thinking in the same way as the half breed, the Virginian had to allow the man to be doubly in his debt. And he had, also, to allow the man the opportunity to discharge the debt. Just as he would have demanded such a chance had the roles of shadowed and shadower been reversed.

And his failure to do this – his act of trying to prevent the man from returning the favour – was what had seeded the self doubt in Steele's mind.

While he did what he always did without sparing a thought for a man who he should have understood as well as he understood himself.

And at last he did.

Joseph Mitchell was going to repay Adam Steele one way or another whatever happened. And what Steele must not do was to help him in any way whatever. For that would only serve to increase the amount of the debt.

It was as simple as that.

The Virginian sighed, spat and then growled : 'Simple is right, Joseph Mitchell. You're hoping I'm riding for a fall so you can catch me. And I'm hoping that happens because it's the only way I'm going to get rid of you. Simple as in brainless.'

He looked back over his shoulder, for the first time since leaving the midday stopover looking for a sight of the half breed. But dusk was falling fast in the wake of the set sun, and although there were many shadows against shadows spread across the terrain behind him, none were moving, nor skylined in the shape of a statue-like man seated astride an immobile horse.

'Yeah,' he murmured after the survey was fruitlessly completed. 'As to the reason for it, Joseph, I'm in the dark, too.'

CHAPTER SEVEN

AN hour later the Virginian glimpsed a gleam of light in the darkness of full night and needed to swing just slightly east from his southerly course to ride directly toward it. Lost sight of the beacon from time to time because of the kind of terrain that intervened. Then, after cresting the low hill that was the final barrier, he was able to look down and see that the light was shining from the window of a small shack.

A single storey, frame built shack with a shade tree in the front yard and neat fields of growing crops to the rear and either side. The unfenced homestead covering no more than four acres.

Steele approached the place from the side, riding across the slope of the hill and along a shallow and slow running stream that bounded the northern extent of the property. Headed the mare up out of the water when he had ridden by a field of beet. To make for the rutted track which curved away from the front of the place, south westward.

The lamp which splashed the light from the window at the side of the shack was doused as the Virginian reached the track: and made to turn the mare on to it. But instead reined the horse to a halt.

Called evenly: 'Hello! I'm passing by is all!'

It had been too quiet on the place, with just the trickling of the stream and the clop of hooves to break what otherwise would be utter silence. Whoever was in the shack would be used to the sound of the running water, but the approach of a rider could not be a routine event in this isolated spot. And so therefore demanded investigation.

Nobody showed at the lighted window to peer out into the night. And nobody made any sound in getting to the door after the lamp was darkened. There was just the metallic click of a latch being raised, heard between two thuds of hooves on hard packed ground, to signal that the shack's door was about to be opened. Which was when Steele reined in the mare and half turned to offer the greeting and assurance. Peered hard between the trunk of the live oak shade tree on one side of the yard and a broken down flatbed wagon on the other to see who was on the threshold of the shack.

'Hello and goodnight, mister. Got no reason to hold you up.'

A woman: her tone of voice as unfriendly as her aggressive stance and the way she aimed a rifle across the yard at the Virginian, its oiled barrel glinting in the moonlight. A tall, broadly built woman. Not young, but neither very elderly. Confident of her ability to defend herself and her property against a lone interloper.

'Ma'am,' Steele acknowledged, and touched the brim of his hat. Made to set the mare moving at the same easy pace as before along the track.

'Mother, that's not being very nice!' a much younger sounding woman complained from immediately behind the aggressively defensive one in the doorway of the shack. 'What's the harm in inviting the gentleman in for a bite of supper and some –'

70

'You ate yet tonight, mister?' Her tone as she cut in on her daughter was only slightly less harsh than before.

'Grateful for the offer, ma'am, but I plan to eat out of my supplies when I bed down on the trail a little later.'

'Nonsense, sir!' the daughter snapped. And pushed between the door jamb and her mother to get out of the house. She was a little shorter and a lot slimmer than the woman who now vented an unladylike snort of annoyance as she stepped off the threshold, too. 'We have so much cold cuts and salad left from our supper and you must stay and help get rid of it.'

She was a long haired blonde in her early twenties. Superficially pretty and with a well proportioned figure attractively contoured by the plain, light coloured dress she wore.

'She's a wilful child, mister. Folks that have dealin's with her all come around to figurin' it's a lot easier to do like she wants than not to.'

She was in her mid-fifties. Blonde, also. Or maybe grey. In the moonlight it was difficult to tell. Her build was more muscular than fat, a dark coloured shirt and dungarees stretched taut across the rises and hollows of her ample form. Perhaps she had been as pretty as her daughter once, for there was a pronounced resemblance between their facial features: but life had had more time to deal heavier blows to the older woman and the ravages of harsh experience had replaced mere good looks with the stamp of character.

'What folks there are to have dealin's with around here!' the daughter said sullenly. Then brightened to

71

plead: 'You will stay, won't you, sir? Eat and sit and talk. Make tonight somethin' different from all the other nights out here in this Godforsaken country?'

'Go set a place at table for him, girl! If I know men, he'll stay. And I used to know men real well. Guess they ain't changed much. I'm Emma Harland, mister. That there's my daughter, Joan. Ain't no Jed Harland no more. Not since three years come July the seventh. You're welcome to come in and stay for awhile. But don't get the idea you can have whatever you want. Jed taught me and his daughter both how to take care of ourselves in the event he was took from us. And, like I told you already, we've had near three years of doin' just that. Ain't got no kind of stock of our own, so there ain't no shelter nor any regular feed for your horse. Hitch him to that old wreck if you want. And I reckon we can get somethin' together for him to eat if it's necessary. Water in the stream if you want to take care of that first. You just come right on in when you're ready, mister. Water for washin' up inside the house.'

Emma Harland kept the Winchester rifle aimed negligently at Steele as she said all this: gesturing with movements of her head when she needed to indicate the shack, a flowerbed at the side of the yard which perhaps was where Jed was buried, the flatbed with two broken wheels, the stream and then the shack again. And she thrust the rifle forward from her hip when she hardened her tone to stress her ability to defend herself.

Joan had relit the lamp and a wedge of light extended across the yard from the open doorway. This· glinted more strongly off the barrel of the Winchester and the woman seemed suddenly to become aware of it as a weapon for the first time in several moments. And she made a sound of self-disgust deep in her throat as she swung around to re-enter the shack – the rifle now down at her side in a one-handed grip.

Steele vented a short, low whistle. Then smiled for a moment – an expression that acted to drop several years from the look of his element burnished face – as he turned further in the saddle to peer across the beet field and the stream to the crest of the long, gentle slope from where he had looked down on the Harland homestead. And where another lone rider sat his stationary horse. Nearer to a half mile than a mile away now. This as the younger woman called:

'Come on, sir! Mother might try to talk you to death, but you don't have anythin' else to be afraid of with us.'

'And if I did, honey,' the Virginian drawled softly as he swung out of the saddle, 'I've got me a guardian angel to watch out for me.'

He led the mare to the tilted over wagon and hitched the reins to the rusted handrail at the side of the seat. Then slid the Colt Hartford from the boot before he turned to go toward the lighted doorway of the shack. Saw that Joseph Mitchell had gone from sight on the hill crest.

'You won't need the rifle,' Emma Harland said sharply from one side of the doorway.

'Where I go, it goes, ma'am,' Steele told her as he entered the shack, and rested the Colt Hartford against the wall: beneath where the Winchester hung on two brackets.

'Okay, but you won't need it. Only peaceable folks live hereabouts.'

She closed the door and vented a soft sigh: as if from satisfaction in a minor chore well done.

'That's mainly because there aren't any folks livin' hereabouts,' Joan said with a tone of bitterness.

The door gave directly on to the parlour of the shack. Which had no window at the front, but the small, undraped one in the side wall which had acted as a beacon to Steele and another in the rear wall. Larger and heavily draped. The dining table was adjacent to the large window, laid with a place for one. One of the two chairs at the table was already pulled out for Steele to sit down.

There were two padded armchairs angled at the sides of a fireplace with an empty grate. Rugs covered much of the floor. Poorly done oil paintings of birds and animals hung on all the walls. And several pieces of unglazed clay sculpture stood on the double decker mantelshelf and overcrowded the top of a sideboard.

'My daughter is an artist, mister,' Emma Harland explained as she took Steele's hat and hung it on the only spare peg behind the door. Lowered her tone to a whisper as she added: 'She cooks better than she works with paint and plaster, young man.'

'Don't whisper, mother!' Joan snapped as she came through the doorway beyond the fireplace. 'It's rude, as you always taught me!'

She carried a plate spread with slices of cold meats and a bowl piled with fresh looking green salad which she placed on the table. Then scowled at her mother, smiled at Steele and held the chair, with a beckoning gesture that he should come and sit on it.

'Grateful to you, Miss Harland,' he said as he crossed to the table and sat at it. Began to pull off the scuffed and torn buckskin gloves.

'You're really welcome, sir. And to call me Joan, if you don't mind.'

'And me Emma, mister,' the older woman urged hurriedly as she came to stand to one side of the table, her daughter having claimed the chair on the other side.

Both of them smiled at the Virginian, then glowered at each other.

'I'm Adam Steele,' he told them, and concentrated on the food: pretended not to be aware of the exchange of tacit animosity between mother and daughter. 'Looks good.'

'So do you, Adam,' Joan said quickly. And giggled, as she dry washed her hands and then folded her arms: like she was afraid of what she might be tempted to do unless she restrained herself. Then, anxiously, added: 'What I mean is, Adam, it's good for us to have a man to tend to again.'

'And how,' Emma Harland put in, a little breathlessly as she clasped her hands behind her back.

Steele chewed and swallowed a mouthful of cold beef and pork and then crunched a scallion. Looked up at each woman in turn and grinned his boyish grin: pretending that he was unaware of the obvious as he said:

'Real glad I allowed myself to be persuaded to come in, ladies. Though at first I had the idea that was the last thing you had in mind.'

'That was mother being all careful, Adam,' Joan said, talking softly to Steele as he pointedly returned his attention to the meal: but did not fail to notice that the girl glared at the older woman again.

'Can you blame me, Adam?' Emma asked and met Joan's look with a matching expression before she directed a smile that was almost simpering at the eating man. 'Me and my little girl livin' out here alone, miles from the nearest neighbour. What else should a mother with such a beautiful daughter do?'

'Heck, mother,' Joan said coyly, then immediately became challenging again. 'She told me to turn out the light and pretend nobody was home. I said you'd already seen the light but –'

'Hell, Adam, soon as I got a close up look at you, I could see you wasn't the kind of man to be afraid of. Even for two women livin' alone out here in the wilderness. Well, it ain't really a wilderness, I guess. The land here supports my daughter and me real well. Lets us raise enough for ourselves with plenty to spare so that we can trade with our neighbours that raises stock and crops we don't grow here. But we are a long way from the nearest of them neighbours, Adam. And sometimes it's real easy to feel like we're the only two folks in the whole wide world.'

Joan had returned to the kitchen and while she was away her mother's attitude became unsubtly altered. She moved around the back of Steele and sat down on the spare chair at the side of the table as she talked, in a tone that got gradually softer and more seductive.

'Ma'am, I –' Steele started, after he had glanced at the woman as she sat down and saw that she was flickering her eyelashes and moistening her lips with a slow moving tongue. Her age making the whole vamping process laughably grotesque.

'I can hear what you're sayin' and how you're sayin' it, you stupid old woman!' Joan called bitingly from the kitchen. 'Ain't you ever gonna learn that it only drives them away?'

Her expression was a match for her tone of voice as she emerged from the kitchen doorway, carrying a plate with a wedge of apple pie on it, and a glass jug of cream.

Her mother turned in the chair to scowl up at Joan with equal viciousness. And snapped: 'Bitch!'

Steele sighed, set down his fork on the plate of half eaten meat and rose. Began to pull on one of the buckskin gloves.

Joan Harland banged down on the table the plate and jug. Her mother got quickly to her feet. And abruptly both wore expressions of desperate pleading.

'What you doin'?'

'Where are you goin'?'

'You haven't finished your supper. There's the pie yet if you don't want the cold cuts!'

'And even if you ain't that hungry you don't have to run so soon!'

'That's right! I can light the stove and make some fresh coffee!'

'I'm grateful for your hospitality, ladies,' the Virginian said as soon as the barrage of questions and suggestions was curtailed. And the two women wrenched their gazes away from his impassive face to stare at each other: looked on the brink of a renewed spat that might go beyond the trading of insults. 'But I reckon I'd best be leaving now.'

He had on both gloves and he turned to move away from the table, intent upon retrieving his rifle and hat.

'Hell, you ain't been here five minutes, mister!' Emma Harland complained, abruptly as angry at him as she ever had been toward her daughter. 'I don't know why you bothered to come visit us if you was only gonna stay this long!'

'It's your damn fault, you stupid old woman!' Joan accused. 'Actin' like you was young and pretty like me! Settin' your cap at him like it was all them years ago when you went courtin' with Pa!'

Steele took his hat off the peg and put it on. Reached down for his rifle with his right hand while his left draped the door latch.

'Touch that gun, Mr Adam Steele and I'll plug you!' Emma Harland warned. 'And you better believe Jed taught me to use this as well as he did the Winchester.'

The Virginian froze his body, but turned his head: to look back over his shoulder and across the room. Saw that the younger woman was where he last saw her – but was smiling instead of frowning. And that her mother had moved away from the table and into the kitchen. Stood in the doorway, aiming a Colt Peacemaker at him: in her right fist held out at arm's length, rock steady. The hammer was cocked with a deliberate movement of her thumb as she finished speaking. Her expression was of grimness tinged with regret.

Steele sighed and straightened up, withdrawing one hand from close to the rifle and dropping the other away from the door latch. Turned slowly to face the two women.

Asked: 'What now?'

'Why'd you come here, mister?'

'You invited me, ma'am.'

'Invited you inside once you reached here,' she corrected sourly. 'How come you rode up to the house?'

'Homed in on your light. Reckoned that where somebody had a house, there was a good chance of there being a trail. Why are you holding a gun on me, Mrs Harland?'

'There's a trail okay,' the older woman said.

'Goes from here to the Widow Perry's place, Adam,' the smiling Joan amplified. 'Ten miles away. And then it's fifteen miles to the next place. Kinda little town there, the places bein' so close on top of each other. The Widow Perry's late husband and my Pa – they didn't like being crowded.'

'Dolly Perry and us get on real fine together, mister. Tradin' back and forth. Not much we have to deal with anybody else for. Anythin' special we get, we share and share alike. And you'll like her, I'm certain of it, mister.'

'Of course, she ain't so young and pretty as me, Adam,' Joan Harland said, and walked a few paces away from the table and back again: her shoulders pulled back to display the full cones of her breasts contoured by the dress bodice, her hips moving in an exaggerated sway. And she tossed her head so that strands of hair fell across her eyes. 'But she's a few years younger than mother. And a whole lot better lookin', I've always thought.'

'Beauty's in the eye of the beholder, girl,' Emma Harland said flatly. 'And anyway, experience can count for a whole lot and make up for a whole lot when a man's lookin' for what he ain't had in a long time.'

'And I guess you ain't, uh Adam?' Joan posed, her stance as seductive as the walk had been. 'Seein' as how this place is so far from anywhere else.'

'What do you say, mister?'

Steele looked from one to the other as they spoke, his expression a thin veneer of impassiveness as he struggled to hold his temper in the face of the threat.

'That I don't believe any of this is happening, Mrs Harland.'

'So make another try to get your rifle and open the door, mister. And see if you'll be able to believe the slug in your belly.'

'She'd plug you easy as she'd step on a roach, Adam,' Joan Harland warned, brushing the blonde hair off her face to be sure that he could see the seriousness of her expression.

'And just what would me being dead do to help you ladies?'

'What you ain't never had, you don't never miss, mister,' the mother said flatly.

And her daughter added: 'But if you wanted it real bad and knew there wasn't no chance of havin' it, helps if you keep other folks from gettin' it.'

The woman with the steadily aimed revolver shook her head and vented a low snort. 'There's been enough talk mister. And out of it all, I figure you got a plain idea what this deal is.'

'Just for awhile, Adam,' Joan urged. 'It'll be so much fun, havin' a man about the place again. And it ain't no lies, what I said about the Widow Perry. She ain't no old hag or nothin' like that. She's a fine lookin' woman, in her face and in her build.'

'Okay,' Steele said.

'What?' Joan countered in surprise.

'He said he agrees, girl,' her mother told her. 'But then so did the last one, and the one before that. To keep from being plugged in the belly. Men lie, girl. Haven't I told you about men so often. How they'll lie through their teeth to take advantage of a woman. But if you want to believe this one, you go ahead, girl. You fall for what he says and give him what he wants from you. You forget about Jed and the evil that he done . . . '

The girl had started to undress as her mother began the dull voiced diatribe against men. First loosened a tie at the waist of her dress, then went down into a crouch, took hold of the hem at both sides and came erect. With an unhurrified deliberateness that gradually obscured her eagerly smiling face while her bare legs were being exposed.

Legs that were pale and shapely; and displayed in such an arousingly sensual manner that for stretched seconds Adam Steele found his attention riveted on the girl. Aware of the aimed gun in the hand of Emma Harland and of the words she spoke. But, despite the danger of the bizarre situation, feeling that he could not drag his gaze away from the ankles, calves, knees and then thighs of the girl. Until, just as it became blatantly obvious Joan Harland wore no under-garments – and that she was a perfectly natural blonde – the name of her father was spoken. In a context that forced the Virginian to look from the daughter to the mother.

And he saw that Emma Harland was smiling – an expression that was mirthless.

Then he switched his curious gaze once more to Joan Harland – as the girl began to sob. Clutching the lower skirt of her dress tightly over her head so that she remained naked from navel to feet.

'I ain't blamin' the girl none, Jed,' Emma Harland said sneeringly. 'She didn't ask to be fetched all the way out here to the middle of nowhere. To a place

81

where there ain't no men closer than twenty-five miles except for her father. And them that's twenty-five miles away is all married and way older than she is. I don't wonder at it that she –'

'No, mother! I didn't want to! Honest, I didn't want to! I didn't know what Pa was gonna do to me! Forgive me, mother! I don't never mean all them things I say about you! Whatever I look like is from you! Maybe Pa's just gone crazy and is thinkin' that I'm you when you was like me!'

'Hush, girl. And cover yourself. On account of it makes it hard for me not to blame you. Way I seen you set out to inflame your father often enough in the past. And now look at you. Displayin' your naked body like a wanton harlot. In front of your own father. This has to stop before it goes too far.'

'Too late, Mother! Already it's too late! Pa made me do this lots of times before!'

Joan Harland was by turns sobbing and laughing. Expressing her emotions to an experience with evil in the past and responding to the good time she was having now. While her mother's mirthless smile grew gradually warmer, broadening as her confidence expanded. Her mind dwelling entirely in the past now, Steele thought. All rationality gone as she was convinced that she was talking to her husband – caught red-handed in the preliminaries of committing incest.

'You gonna deny that, Jed?' Emma Harland asked. And for the first time, her gun hand wavered a little. But with excitement rather than rage or nervousness – as she relished the prospect of again ending the life of a man she obviously abhorred.

'No, Emma,' Steele said coldly. 'I can't deny it.

Because I'm only a man. And look at her. You spoke the truth, woman. She's nothing but a wanton harlot.'

The Virginian was convinced he was aware of every bead of sweat squeezing from each of his pores. Pasting his clothing to his flesh and standing out on his exposed skin. This as he shifted his gaze from mother to daughter – the one aiming the gun at him while the other continued to inch the dress higher. To an extent where the lower halves of her breasts were uncovered now. While Joan sobbed and wailed, her deranged mind taken back entirely to the same plane of the past as that where her mother was presently existing.

'If I deserve to be punished, woman, then so does she!' Steele went on. 'If I'm bad, so is she! Look at her, woman! Look at the way she's flaunting her naked body – '

He knew he could be within a second of being shot to death with each word he spoke – as he stared with ice cold eyes out of a sweat beaded face at the slender body of the girl. While on the periphery of his vision he had a blurred image of the woman with the gun. Knew without needing to concentrate on her face that she was staring straight at him.

Knew when she began to shift her head over the first fraction of an inch – to start to look at her daughter's nakedness. And realised that this was to be his only chance.

His eyes flicked across the sockets. And now the nude body of Joan, both breasts totally free of the dress, was out of focus. While he saw the time and careworn face of her mother in stark clarity as, for just a part of a second, her entire attention was captured by the naked girl.

The Peacemaker in the fist of the older woman moved almost imperceptibly to one side. This as Emma Harland endured a moment's doubt. Then her mouth gaped wide, her eyes squeezed closed and sprang open. Her head swung so that she was staring directly at Steele again.

'No, it was your fault!' she screamed at a shrill pitch. 'Like the first time, you have to die, Jed!'

Steele was going down and to the side as she shrieked at him. His right hand delving into the gaping slit in the leg of his pants.

Then the undraped window suddenly shattered to spray shards of glass into the room.

And both the women and he snapped their heads around at the sound of smashing glass: and the crack of a gunshot. Looked from the window to the girl. Who took two paces to the side, banged into the chair Steele had used and fell backwards across it. No longer making any sound. The dress still draping her head and shoulders. Blood trickling from a hole in the lower slope of her left breast. A much larger amount of blood stained the floor, having gushed from the ragged exit wound in the wake of the killing bullet.

Joseph Mitchell complained: 'Aw shit, I plugged the wrong crazy woman!'

His voice dispelled the shock which had held Adam Steele and Emma Harland immobile in the wake of watching the naked girl's death tumble.

'You bastard, Jed, you bastard, you bastard, you shot her!' the woman shrieked.

But no longer was the Virginian mistaken for her long dead incestuous husband. Instead, the half breed outside the glassless window was on the spot –

as he showed himself plainly in the lamplight. Thrust the barrel of Vic Judd's Springfield rifle into the room. Ordered, with his lips moving on the top of the stock:

'Drop the pistol, woman. Or you'll get the next bullet!'

Emma Harland vented a short, sharp, very shrill laugh that dripped with contempt: as she continued to turn from the waist and track the Peacemaker on to a fresh target.

'You're so blinded by lust for your own daughter you can't think straight, Jed!' she accused as the Colt's arc was halted. 'Why, if I ain't mistaken, husband, that's the same Springfield we had when we first come to this rotten place. Single shot is all. First rifle you taught me to shoot with. Before the Win —'

Steele maybe had time to switch his plan – abandon going for the knife in the boot sheath to turn and reach for the Colt Hartford leaning against the wall. Time certainly to get shot off at Emma Harland before she could recollect he was there and swing her handgun back to aim it at him. But since he was committed to draw and throw the knife, it offered the best chance of stopping her triggering a bullet at Joseph Mitchell.

The knife came clear of the sheath and out through the slit in the pants. At first tightly and then loosely gripped by the right gloved fist of the Virginian.

The arm went back fast and came forward faster while Steele remained in a half crouch. All this before the Colt Peacemaker drew a bead on the suddenly terrified half breed.

But then Emma Harland adjusted her aim as she

taunted the man she thought was her husband. Tilted the revolver so that the muzzle moved its menace from Mitchell's chest to his belly. Now gripped the gun butt in both hands.

The knife was released by then. To be sent spinning along a rising trajectory from the gloved hand of the fully extended arm. Blade glinting in the lamplight.

With the woman on the threshold of the kitchen holding the Peacemaker fully out in front of her from the shoulder in a double handed grip, her sideways-on torso was totally exposed as a target for the throwing knife.

The point stabbed into her left flank at the base of her breast. The force with which the knife had been powered driving the blade deep into the flesh. Between two bones of the ribcage. To puncture a lung.

Steele vented a soft curse when he realised he had missed his target of her heart.

The woman curtailed what she was saying to Mitchell and wrenched her head down to stare at the handle, hilt and part of the blade of the knife protruding from her side. Gasped with the shock of the impact.

The half breed gave a cry of alarm and threw himself to the ground, out of the line of fire should the still fully extended revolver explode a shot.

It was too early for the wound to be painful. But there was a deep hurt in the eyes of Emma Harland as she looked up from the knife in her side to gaze at Adam Steele.

She rasped: 'Dear God in heaven —'

Gagged on the blood which welled up from the

punctured lung to flood salty warmth into her throat.

She recognised the Virginian as a man not her husband. Stared at the glassless window from which another man who was not her husband had gone from sight. Then, more slowly, shifted her gaze to the nude body of her daughter draped obscenely over the chair.

She tried to scream. But the blood in her throat checked the sound as it entered her mouth. And spilled over her lower lip. And then she fell forward. Stiffly like a toppling tree. And the crack of a bullet involuntarily blasted from the gun into the floor might have been the splitting of the timber as the trunk tore free of the stump.

Full length on the floor, fully clothed and faced down close to the differently sprawled corpse of her daughter, the woman twitched and moaned for several seconds — crimson spurting from her frenetically working mouth — before the limpness of death took a grip on her ample form.

By then the Virginian had picked up his rifle and canted it to his shoulder. And as soon as Emma Harland was still, he moved across the room. Was stooped down and drawing the knife out of her when the half breed became framed at the smashed window again.

He scowled as he said: 'What a damn waste.'

'Of what, feller?' the Virginian asked as he wiped the blade clean of blood on the dead woman's shirt before he slid it back in the sheath. And stood up.

'I figure I maybe saved your skin when I fired the shot into this place. No matter which of these crazy women I hit. But you sure as hell kept me from goin' to the happy huntin' ground again. When you stuck her with that blade just when she was gonna blast at me. And one cancels out the other, Mr Steele. The way I see it.'

The Virginian reached over the chair across which Joan Harland was draped and made a point of not looking at her as he picked up the piece of apple pie she had brought from the kitchen for him. Took a bite of it and chewed the good tasting food as he went toward the door.

'Figure you have to see it that way as well, Mr Steele,' the half breed said, very anxious to have the other man's agreement.

'And we both reckoned they were crazy,' Steele growled as he swallowed some pie and opened the door.

'From what I seen and heard, crazy as they come,' Mitchell countered, puzzled.

'They don't have any more problems now though,' Steele answered as he stepped out of the shack, taking another bite of pie.

'Shit, nobody'd rather be dead!' the half breed yelled after him.

The Virginian closed the door on the man at the window and went to his horse. Murmured through a mouthful of food: 'Seems like that's the only way most people ever get to rest in peace.'

CHAPTER EIGHT

ADAM Steele finished the pie before he unhitched the mare from the wagon with the broken wheels and swung up astride the saddle. Rode out of the moon shadow of the live oak and reined in the horse at the point where the rutted track began.

Looked back over his shoulder, but not at the shack with a wedge of yellow lamplight pointing out of the open doorway across the yard. Instead, toward the hill slope north of the Harland homestead. Where Joseph Mitchell sat astride the gelding of Vic Judd, occupied with the process of reloading the single shot Springfield. Then, when Mitchell glanced up after sliding the reloaded rifle into the boot, the Virginian raised a hand and beckoned to him.

The half breed paused, as if he needed to be certain that he did not mistake the other man's intention. Then thudded in his heels to gallop the gelding across the slope, did not break pace as water from the stream was flung high, and skilfully slowed his mount to close up with and move alongside the mare which Steele had started forward.

'Did I tell you thanks for what you did, Joseph?' the Virginian asked of the half breed with the features of an Apache and the pallor of a white. Who was finding it hard to control his excitement at being invited to ride with Steele.

'Ain't no need for that. Still owe you two.'

'You have the gold, feller?'

Mitchell was abruptly suspicious and disappointed as he snapped his head around to stare at the man riding beside him: his face in the frame of the jet black hair now devoid of any trace of suppressed joy.

'You want it, Mr Steele? If you want it, you can have it. But it won't make no difference to me owin' you.'

He was totally the child-like white man now, in attitude, tone of voice and expression. Submissively docile, like a cruelly trained animal that needs to have commands with which to comply.

'I didn't even steal that piece of apple pie back there, Joseph,' the Virginian answered after the briefest of glances at his riding companion. 'Reckon I can't claim that I never stole anything from anybody. But I'm no –'

Now Mitchell was unable to control a short burst of laughter, as his joy at being invited to ride with Steele was resurrected and merged with relief that the Virginian did not have any financial motive in calling him forward.

'Shit, that's real fine, sir! And I guess I'm a fool for doubtin' you! I've knowed you was okay from the time you hauled me outta the quicksand. Maybe before that – when you didn't take no shot at me back on that beach when you first seen me. You've treated me real well, Mr Steele. And a man like that – who don't act toward a half Apache like he's lower than horseshit, well . . . he ain't the kind to turn right around and take from me all I got to give me a fresh start.'

'Bad's not fresh, feller,' Steele said, and his tone

90

matched the note of sincere earnestness with which the other man finished.

'Uh?' Mitchell grunted, with a puzzled frown as he imitated Steele's actions of reining in his mount.

'You know what's down this trail, feller?'

The Virginian nodded to indicate the little used track cut with ancient wheel ruts that curved and rose and dipped across the lush green rolling country spread to the south and west of where they sat their halted horses.

'That crazy woman said there was another widow woman's place and then some kinda small town, didn't she?'

'That, sure,' Steele allowed. 'But a whole lot more. Other places and other towns and other trails. And maybe there'll be someplace where nobody will think there's anything strange about a half breed showing up out of nowhere with a thousand dollars in gold dust. A place where –'

'Mr Steele,' Mitchell cut in quietly.

'Yes?'

'I ain't stupid, sir. I ain't the smartest half Apache in this country, but I ain't the dumbest, either. Soon as our business is over and done with, I have plans. Same plans I was workin' on while I was waitin' my chance to blast Ethan Winston and get the gold.'

Steele shrugged and heeled the mare into an easy walk again, feeling a little cold in the brightly moonlit night: but not so much that he could be bothered to take the sheepskin coat from his bedroll and put it on. For soon it would be time to make night camp.

Mitchell was lost in reflective thought about his plan and was taken by surprise when the Virginian moved off. But was only half a horse length behind. Waited until they were precisely side by side though before he continued:

'I'm gonna find a place where grubbers panned gold before but now is all worked out. And I'm gonna stake a claim and stay on it a long time. Then show up in the closest town with the dust. Tell folks that I panned it.'

He finished on a high note, as if he fully expected the Virginian to be impressed with what he had been told. And when no kind of response was forthcoming, he asked in an indifferent tone:

'You don't figure it'll work, uh?'

'Reckon it could work, feller,' Steele corrected. 'But that won't make the gold yours anymore than it would if you walked into any bank in any town and deposited it, Joseph.'

'I know that! Don't you think I know that, Mr Steele?'

He was abruptly sullen and remained so for several minutes after Steele had again failed to answer him. Then, eventually, the half breed challenged:

'Back when you blasted Vic Judd and Ryan King, you told me the dust was most likely on Judd's horse. You said I should take it. And forget everythin' that happened after I blasted Ethan Winston. Didn't you say all that, Mr Steele?'

The Virginian had angled the mare off the trail, in another move that took the half breed by surprise while he was deep in thought.

'Sure, feller,' Steele agreed as he halted the mare beside a small pool on the fringe of a stand of timber and swung wearily down from the saddle. 'And if you had done all of that, you wouldn't be tagging along with me now.'

He began to unsaddle the horse as the half breed dismounted on the trail and led the gelding by the reins.

'On account that maybe you wouldn't be around to tag along with, did you think of that? On account of you'd still be back at that place with the crazy women. Them alive and you dead.' He vented a deep sigh as he began to take the saddle off his horse. Then growled: 'Aw shit, Mr Steele. I got no call to be mad with you.'

'You know something, feller?' the Virginian said as he moved into the timber to collect dead-wood for a fire.

'I've always been ready and willin' to learn.'

'You have the right to be anything or do anything you want. Providing it's not against the law.'

'That's easy for a full white man in a white man's country to say,' Joseph Mitchell muttered as Steele emerged from the deep shadows under the trees with an armful of firewood.

Yet again, the Virginian responded with silence. And this time the half breed changed the subject to fill the pause as the other man crouched to start building a fire.

'That won't be enough, Mr Steele. I'll go bring some more.'

Mitchell was gone for a long time to collect not much more dead-wood than Steele brought. Long enough for the fire to be well alight and for the steam rising from the coffee pot to be aromatic with the smell of fresh grounds.

'Sorry I was away so long. Needed to crap.'

'We all get full of it sometimes,' Steele allowed from where he sat on his saddle on the far side of the fire from the pool, the sheepskin coat draped over his shoulders. 'Had enough to eat at the Harland place. Just boiling up some coffee. You want to cook anything, go right ahead.'

Mitchell set down the bundle of wood and shook his head. Made iike he was about to hunker down on his gear, but then began to pace back and forth: just as he did on the beach in the early morning.

'I ain't hungry, but some coffee won't come amiss, Mr Steele. I been thinkin'.'

The Virginian poured himself some coffee and asked: 'Pass your cup, feller.'

The pacing man, moving along a ten stride line that came into and out of the aura of light from the fire, shook his head again.

'Later. You know how old I am? Fifty-three is how old I am. Yet a lot of people treat me like I'm seven years old. Maybe on account of that's how old I act a lot of the time. Ain't gonna be that way no more. And I'd appreciate it if you'd quit talkin' to me like I just climbed down off my Ma's knee.'

He came to an abrupt halt, his face brightly lit by the fire's glow as he peered through the smoke and heat shimmer at the Virginian – a face hard set in an expression of determined resolution. Which did not alter in a single line as he qualified:

'Not that I don't understand you been meanin' well toward me.'

Steele answered across the cup clasped in both gloved hands: 'Sure, Joseph.'

'Wouldn't have got around to thinkin' this way if it hadn't been for you.'

Steele merely inclined his head in acknowledgement this time. And the half breed grunted and recommenced to pacing again. And speaking aloud the thoughts he was reconsidering.

'A kid, he ain't never proud of nothin' he does unless the grown-ups pat him on the head and tell him he has good reason to be proud. But for a man, it's a whole lot different. When a man has reason to feel pride, it don't matter a shit what other folks think. And there's nothin' I ever done before in my adult life give me a greater respect for myself than when I blasted a hole in Ethan Winston, Mr Steele. And it don't matter that I shot the sonofabitch in the back,'

He paused briefly, with the talk and with the pacing. But then recalled he had claimed it no longer mattered to him what anybody else thought of his actions. And grinned with the pride of which he had been speaking.

'He treated me bad. Tried to get me lynched for his killin' and stealin'. And it was just for me alone I lost them vigilantes, tracked down Ethan Winston and killed him. For the Apache part of me, Mr Steele. The part that figured, if I was gonna be wanted for somethin' I didn't do . . . then, shit, I'd do it and benefit outta it. Have that coffee now, okay?'

He stopped beside his pile of gear, took Vic Jedd's cup from out of Vic Judd's bedroll and came to sit on his haunches beside the fire. Poured coffee into the cup and remained hunkered down, close to Steele but peering into the glowing ashes.

'And if you hadn't showed up, that's just what I'd have done. Took off and tried to make that new start the way I told you. But you're right.' He shook his head, the gesture, the expression on his face and his tone of voice all conveying self disgust. 'It would've been a bad way to make a new start. And I don't mean on account of never bein' able to look over my shoulder without bein' scared of seein' somebody who remembered me from Golden Hill, Mr Steele. I mean of not bein' able to look in a mirror and forgettin' I shot down a man in cold blood for the gold he was carryin'.'

He sipped at his coffee and continued to peer at the ashes and the small tongues of flame that rose from them.

'Whether I saw the Apache part or the white part in me,' he added after several seconds of easy silence. 'On account of I want it to be that I ain't never ashamed of . . . aw shit, I figure you got my point?'

'Sure, Joseph,' Steele replied as the other man eyed him with an expression that came close to embarrassment. 'And it raises another one.'

Mitchell looked hard at the Virginian now and, with the red glow from the fire burnishing his cheeks and jaw and brow, he appeared at that moment like a full blooded Apache brave.

'I'm stickin' with you!' he said, voice as grim as the look on his very Indian face. 'Until I'm out of your debt. Then I'll take care of what I have to do to square myself with the folks back at Golden Hill.'

'You all through, feller?'

'Uh?'

'You've done one hell of a lot of talking.'

Mitchell shrugged. 'You did your share earlier on. Enough to make me see I was ridin' for another fall.'

Steele nodded as he took a final swig of the coffee, jerked out the grounds and set down the cup. Began to unfurl his bedroll as he said:

'The other point it raises is the one where the talking has to stop, Joseph.'

'I know that. Don't you think I know that, Mr Steele?' He threw some more fuel on the fire. 'Ain't I just said that as soon as our business is done, then I plan on –'

'Heading on back to Golden Hill and allowing them to lynch you, feller. If they don't shoot you on sight.'

The Virginian had spread the bedroll and placed his saddle at one end to serve as a pillow. Now, fully dressed in his suit and boots, he got under a blanket with the sheepskin coat on top. And, as always, had his right hand fisted to the frame of the Colt Hartford. With his free hand he placed his hat over his face to blot out the light of the moon, the stars and the fire as Joseph Mitchell countered:

'Least I won't die runnin' away from anythin'.'

'That's being pretty damn hard on me, Joseph,' Steele told him.

'On you?'

'Means I'll have been saving you so that others can waste you.'

CHAPTER NINE

ONCE again Adam Steele enjoyed a night of the kind of rest that he had last evening cynically claimed was allowed only to the dead. And did not awaken until the bright, warm rays of the California sun lanced down over the ridges of the inland mountains and infiltrated his eyelids beneath the brim of his hat. Woke to the smell of cooking pork and beans and simmering coffee and the sound of a crackling fire – then the voice of a man demanding to know:

'Where'd the Injun go, mister?'

A prod with the toe of a boot rather than a kick against the ribs accompanied the question. At the same time as the Stetson was knocked off Steele's face by the muzzle of a Winchester. Which was immediately withdrawn when the questioner stepped back three paces. To then halt and hold the rifle across the base of his belly.

The Virginian blinked against the glare of the newly risen sun and then moved just his head. Raised it slightly off the saddle and turned it first to the left, next to the right. Saw that the man who had roused him was standing beside another who held a Winchester rifle in a similar manner. While perhaps two paces further removed on the other side of where he lay stood a man and a woman.

'Ma'am,' he greeted. 'Gentlemen.'

'Just answer the friggin' question, squirt!' the

woman snapped. 'And cut the rest of the cackle!'

She was in her early forties or was perhaps a well preserved fifty and some. Full figured without any suggestion of fat. With good, strong features and jet black hair. Not looking her feminine best this morning in the kind of work boots, dungarees and shirt Emma Harland had worn. Plus a Stetson with a floppy brim.

'He's just a half Indian and I don't know where he's gone,' Steele answered, not showing any reaction to the strangeness of his awakening.

'Now, now, Dolly,' the elderly, thin stoop shouldered, grey haired man in work clothes who stood beside her placated. 'I don't believe there's any excuse for that kind of language even though —'

'And you can cut the cackle, too, Lloyd Weeks!' the woman snarled at him. 'You, squirt! You and the breed or whatever he is was at the Harland place last night! Ain't no use denyin' it, 'cause we know! Phil Tucker and Moses Jackson been huntin' all their lives and they can track better'n any —'

'We ain't here to talk huntin', Dolly,' the man who had prodded Steele growled. He was still on the right side of fifty. Tall and broad and in good shape. With dark eyes, hair and skin tones. Dressed in fur trimmed jacket, fur lined boots with his pants cuffs tucked inside and a coon hat. 'I'm Jackson, stranger. And this here is Phil Tucker. You wanna give us your name?'

'Shit, what is this?' the woman snarled. 'A church friggin' picnic is what it's startin' to sound like it is!'

'What it's gettin' to sound like to me, Dolly Perry,' the third man said evenly, 'is that it's a waste of time me and Moses and Lloyd being' out here. Seein' as how you figure you can take care of what needs to be done.'

Tucker was dressed in a similar style of hunting gear to Jackson, except that his coat had more fur trim. He was about thirty-five. Less tall and not so powerfully built as the older man at his side. But with a face that was more weather beaten, like he had spent more time in far tougher conditions out of doors than had Tucker. His eyes were ice blue and his hair was blond. He had not shaved for several days, but for a constructive reason – the bristles had been trimmed into the shape of an embryo beard.

His clear eyed gaze shifted from the scowling face of the woman to the impassive one of Steele as he grunted his satisfaction with the Widow Perry's angry silence.

'I ain't quite so impatient as Dolly, stranger,' he said, expression as implacable as that of the Virginian. 'But I don't plan on wastin' the whole day out here. You was at the Harland house, wasn't you?'

'Right, feller,' Steele admitted as he wriggled into a half sitting posture against the saddle. And reached with his left hand to retrieve and put on his hat. While his right hand remained out of sight beneath the blanket and the sheepskin coat, still fisted around the frame of the Colt Hartford.

'And how were Emma and Joan when you left the house?' Moses Jackson asked nervously, blinking a great deal and shuffling his feet.

From his slightly different viewpoint, Steele could see that the fire had been recently built-up with fresh fuel. And across the fire with its cooking and coffee pots, the half breed's bedroll was still unfurled and rumpled from being slept in.

His mare and Mitchell's gelding were still hobbled at the side of the pool, calmly cropping at the lush grass in the morning shade of the stand of timber.

'Dead, feller.'

'Oh, dear,' the elderly Lloyd Weeks murmured.

'Breed done it, did he, squirt?' Dolly Perry snapped eagerly. 'Injuns and breeds, there ain't nothing to choose between them when it comes to them tryin' to make it with white women.'

'Joseph shot the daughter,' Steele confirmed. 'I had to use my knife on Emma Harland, ma'am.'

The Virginian did not look toward the widow and the shocked man beside her as he gave his even voiced reply. Instead, concentrated on the two men with rifles. While, on the periphery of his vision, he was able to watch an area of trees across the pool in back of them. Where the half breed was undoubtedly hiding – with the Springfield rifle of a dead man.

'Son-of-a-bitch,' Moses Jackson rasped softly with a distinct pause between each word. And took a knuckle whitening tighter grip on his Winchester. Did not shift its position, though.

'Who the hell else, Moses?' the unaffected Phil Tucker growled, gazing fixedly at Steele. 'How many strangers use this trail? When was the last time?' He spat out of the side of his mouth into the edge of the fire. 'Looks like he's taken a powder and left you to take the rap for both killin's, stranger.'

'Typical, for a friggin' Injun!' the woman snarled. 'Can't trust the stinkin' bastards any further than you can kick their asses! And you're crazy, squirt! Ownin' up to stickin' the knife in Emma Harland! If you'd said the Injun half breed had done both murders, we'd have likely swallowed — '

'You would have, Dolly,' Jackson cut in grimly. And now swung the Winchester to level it at Steele from his hip – a thumb on the uncocked hammer. 'Bein' prejudiced the way you are. But we got to do this thing the legal way. Right, Phil?'

'You're the deputy when needs be,' the younger man agreed – and tracked his rifle on to the same target of the Virginian's deadpan face. But he thumbed back the hammer.

'You never did give your name, mister?' Jackson reminded.

'Adam Steele. Deputy from where?'

'Six Rivers County, Mr Steele. Which is what you're in now. Same as the Harland place is in it. You're under arrest and I'm gonna take you in.'

'In where?'

'Fort Trinity where the sheriff has his office and gaol, Mr Steele. And a court house where the circuit judge will see you get a fair trial. But that's a two day ride from here. Figure we'll have to keep you under guard in my barn at the valley tonight.'

'Shit, Moses Jackson!' the widow woman exploded. 'He's a confessed murderer! You don't have to talk to him like he's some honoured friggin' guest of the county!'

'Innocent until proved guilty, Dolly,' Jackson murmured.

'Deputy sheriff,' the woman growled softly. 'Horse's ass.'

'This is somethin' entirely new to all of us, my dear,' Lloyd Weeks said in a conciliatory tone. 'I don't think you have any call to —'

'Go jerk yourself off!' she flung at him. 'Which is what you all can do. Forever, far as I'm concerned!

Because you sure as hell ain't none of you ever gonna get under the sheets with me again! I'm a woman who needs a man! And, far as I'm concerned, there's more to bein' a man than havin' what it takes to screw a woman!'

She spun around and strode angrily away. To the trail and across it. Down into a hollow on the other side.

'Dolly, you can't go off alone with a hostile Injun on the loose around here!' Weeks called after her.

Then, desperation in his eyes, he stared at Steele for a moment and Jackson and Tucker for a little longer. Back at the man on the ground when the Virginian drawled:

'Compared to the women in this area, feller, Joseph's as easy to get along with as a —'

'I'm goin' after her!' Lloyd Weeks snapped.

And did so, hurrying in what looked like it could be a painful gait in the wake of the embittered woman who was now out of sight down in the hollow.

' . . . me on a good day,' Steele finished. 'All right to have breakfast before we leave?'

If both men with levelled rifles had switched their attention toward the half running Weeks, the Virginian would have taken his chance to get the drop on them. But only the anxious deputy sheriff was distracted by this side issue. Tucker continued to peer fixedly at the Virginian, his light blue eyes as unwavering as the dark muzzle of the tightly gripped Winchester.

'The Widow Perry ain't never been no different ever since she first came out here, Mr Steele,' Jackson explained dully, ruefully and a little absently as he returned his nervous gaze to the Virginian. 'Used to cheat on her husband when he was alive. And after Jim died she become nothin' more nor less than the valley whore. Ain't makin' no excuses for her. She wouldn't make none for herself. She's the way she is and there's an end to it.'

'Damnit, Moses, this ain't nothin' to this saddle-tramp Injun lover,' Tucker complained. Seemingly intent upon vocalising his toughness every now and again as a counterpoint to the urbane attitude of the deputy sheriff. Perhaps, Steele reflected as he watched for a sign of it, as a cover for a brand of nervousness that was more insidious than that affecting Jackson.

Then the sign was heard instead of seen. When the older man shot a curious glance at Tucker and said:

'I never knew you had any strong feelin's against Indians, Phil?'

'Hell, I ain't!' He swallowed hard and then spat into the fire again. 'Unless one of them is gunnin' for me. And we can't be sure this one just took off on the run. He could be some place close, waitin' for a chance to jump us.' Yet another spit into the fire while the man's blue eyes remained in their fixed stare at Steele's face. 'But this is for sure! If he does try anythin', you won't live to see how it comes out, stranger!'

Moses Jackson was moved to fear of the half breed by Phil Tucker's hoarsely spoken words. Glanced over his shoulder at the stand of timber, across the trail to the hollow into which the Widow Perry and Lloyd Weeks had gone: then back at Steele. There was no cover along the northern stretch of trail and on the area to the west of it for several hundred yards.

'What do you think, Mr Steele?' Moses Jackson asked earnestly and the Winchester he held wandered off target – as if he had forgotten he was holding a rifle.

'I was asleep, feller. Woke up maybe a second and a half before you knocked the hat off my face.'

The deputy who was obviously not relishing his official position, shook his head and displayed an expression of irritation for a moment.

'I've accepted your word on that. I honestly believe you don't know where he's gone. But you're ridin' with him, Steele. I guess you know him. What would he do in this kind of situation, do you think?'

'Shit, Moses, I —' Tucker started.

'Hold it, Phil! Let the man speak. Go ahead, Steele.'

'What kind of situation is it, feller?'

'Uh?' Jackson frowned. 'Look, if you wanna horse around, I can just . . .'

He was lost for a course of action to threaten. And Steele spoke before the truculent Tucker even had the time to open his mouth.

'I bedded down and went to sleep here last night with just Joseph Mitchell for company. And the next thing I knew, I was waking up with four strangers around me.'

'Killin' defenceless women what it takes to give you a good night's rest, stranger?' Phil Tucker taunted.

'I killed just the one and she wasn't defenceless, feller,' Steele answered, his tone of voice still even and his expression calm in the face of the other man's ire. 'And from the way he's handlin' this, I reckon the lawman here has a good idea there's more to it than you're trying to make out, feller?'

The Virginian looked far to the left and right, as if as part of the gesture of shrugging his shoulders to express his confusion. And in so doing failed to see any sign of the half breed. Or the Perry woman and Lloyd Weeks. When he returned his undivided attention to the two men with levelled Winchesters, Jackson was still discomfitted and Tucker appeared not to trust himself to speak.

Steele went on: 'And if you knew there was somebody else here at the night camp, how come you let him get away?'

'That was last night, Mr Steele,' the reluctant deputy explained, using the courtesy title again. 'Phil and me were out huntin'. Called in at the Widow Perry's to rest up an . . . well, she was entertainin' Weeks —'

'Shit, Moses, why you tellin' him all this?' Tucker snarled. 'If Flora and Rose find out we was at —'

'What the hell?' Jackson exploded shrilly, his expression altering from a worried frown to a mask of horror as his attention was wrenched away from what the younger man was saying to some activity on the trail.

The Virginian felt compelled by the sudden change in the man's attitude and the depth of feeling in his voice and expression to look in the same direction.

And a part of a second later, so did Phil Tucker.

Thus did all three men for an immeasurably short period of time have their eyes focussed upon the grisly tableau that the half Apache Joseph Mitchell set before them.

Before two gunshots ended the lives of two of the trio.

107

The Widow Perry and Lloyd Weeks were already dead: the awesome evidence of their passing the cause of the shock that for that briefest part of a second froze into helpless immobility the three men beside the cooking fire on the fringe of the timber.

It was not possible to see how the couple had died. For Joséph Mitchell chose to display only the severed heads of his victims. Each skewered by the bloodied neck wound on to the end of a two pronged bough. Which the half breed held thrust high into the morning air in his right hand – the hand and wrist and sleeve of the shirt encasing his arm stained with the blood that had spilled from the terrible wounds and dripped down on to him.

Then, at the instant he knew his horrific display had captured and frozen his three man audience, the blood stained man threw his right arm forward, his grip on the bough as firm as ever. So that the pair of heads were hurtled off the prongs to arc toward the watchers. Hair streaming and blood drops spraying in the slipstream through the bright and suddenly overheated air of early morning.

'Oh, my God!' Moses Jackson shrieked as he saw the heads fly free.

'I don't friggin' believe —' Phil Tucker started.

Joseph Mitchell had been carrying a Winchester rifle in his left hand. Took a two handed grip on the gun as he let go of the bough. Dropped into a half crouch, turned sideways-on, and thudded the stock of the rifle to his shoulder. Squeezed the trigger and blasted a bullet between the falling heads.

Pumped the lever action of the repeater and fired again.

So that before the severed heads hit the ground

and Jackson and Tucker had time to recover from the shock of what they saw, the two men were also dead. From close range rifle shots that tunnelled bullets through their hearts and out of their backs. Each of them corkscrewing to the ground, his unfired Winchester slipping from out-of-control hands.

This was what the half breed saw as his frown of concentration altered to a grin of satisfaction. But then, as the heads thudded to the ground and the frames of Jackson and Tucker started to collapse, his mind registered the certain fact that the two gunshots had been echoed.

In the kind of country that had no nearby rock faces off which sound could be bounced.

And he wrenched his eyes across their sockets, anger lighting them and lips curling to switch the mouthline from a grin to a scowl.

Twin wisps of smoke curled up from holes in the sheepskin coat that contoured the lower half of Adam Steele — perhaps a half inch between the scorched rim of each hole in the fabric.

Mitchell powered forward then — across the rutted trail and the grassy area to the camp. Halted with his bare feet between the blood spattered heads of Dolly Perry and Lloyd Weeks. To gaze through the smoke and distorting heat shimmer of the fire at the faces of the two men attired for hunting. Vented a choked snarl of frustration when he saw that each man had a bullet hole beneath his jaw — and that each of the coon skin hats they wore was starting to become damply stained from the insides.

'Aw, shit,' he groaned as disappointment drained the energy for anger out of him. And his shoulders sagged, his arms dropped to his sides and the high colour left the flesh of his face so that it was pallid again. 'I had them for sure that time!'

'Sure you did,' the Virginian drawled.

'There ain't no way to be so sure of that!'

'I didn't head anybody off, feller.'

'But you shot —'

'You finished them, seems to me,' Steele cut in on him as he withdrew the Colt Hartford from beneath the blanket and sheepskin. And flicked open the loading gate to extract the two spent shells. 'All I did was undercoat them.'

CHAPTER TEN

STEELE ate a plateful of pork and beans while Joseph Mitchell got rid of the corpses: first tossed the severed heads into the timber, then dragged the unmutilated bodies of Jackson and Tucker deep through the brush. Went across the trail and down into the hollow to bring up and conceal the rest of the Widow Perry and Lloyd Weeks.

The Virginian drank a cup of coffee while he ate breakfast and was midway through a second cup when the half breed returned. Spooned some breakfast out of the pot himself and asked as he sat down on his saddle to eat:

'Don't you want to ask me how it all come to happen, Mr Steele?'

'When we're riding.'

He threw away the dregs from his cup and then moved to squat beside the pool: washed all he had dirtied at breakfast.

'We should get outta here fast, you figure?'

'I reckon we should get out of here, Joseph. But don't bolt the pork and beans. Bad for the digestion.'

Steele shaved in cold water from the pool. And then the half breed attended to the cooking and coffee pots. While Steele doused the fire. Then both acted in concert to saddle their horses, furl their bedrolls and stow their gear.

'One of them say somethin' that made you figure

other folks'll be comin' by here soon, Mr Steele?'
Mitchell asked, voicing a concern that had been
apparent during the lengthy silence while the men
were preparing to leave camp.

The Virginian had been his usual impassive self.
And remained so as he swung into the saddle,
answered:

'No, feller. Two of them were hunting, two were
screwing. Just plain bad luck got them to the wrong
place at the wrong time. I just don't want that kind of
luck to happen to any other innocent homesteaders
who come riding by here for whatever reason.'

'Anyone who tries to kill me ain't innocent, far as
I'm concerned,' the half breed rasped from astride
his horse. And tugged on the reins and moved his
bare heels against the gelding's flanks to ride
alongside the Virginian. 'And it can't be denied
that's what they wanted to do. Not here and now
maybe. But in some town after a trial. Which would
be a waste of time. With a white judge and white jury
and me a half breed.'

Steele was dictating the pace and direction of the
ride – a slow walk across the trail and then over the
rolling pastureland spread to the north east. Skirting
the rim of the hollow in which four horses, saddled
and unhobbled, were cropping at the lush grass.

'Town of Fort Trinity which is two day's ride from
here, Joseph,' the Virginian supplied. 'And I'm not
blaming you for anything that happened. Was due to
spend time in the gaol and courthouse of Fort Trinity
myself. And was waiting for you to make your move.
If you hadn't, then I would have had to make a play
of my own.'

'Without killin' them, uh?' the half breed came

back quickly and was child-like again in sullenness – wore the expression of a small boy bawled out for an action undertaken in good faith with the highest intentions.

'Forget it, feller.'

'I don't wanna forget it, Mr Steele. I owe you my life and I'm tryin' to pay you back. And if you think I'm doin' you wrong to pay you back, then it ain't no good at all.'

Steele spat to the side, opposite that on which Joseph Mitchell rode. Then he glanced for perhaps a second into the heavily bristled, Indian featured face in its frame of jet black hair. And grimaced in response to the intensely quizzical frown the half breed was directing at him.

He faced front again – peering far across the rolling country to where the ridges of the distant mountains were already blurred by a shimmering heat haze. And said:

'In the easy art of killing, feller, you've only just started in the first grade. And I graduated from that school a long time ago. Sure I would have killed that deputy and the others. And not as a last resort to keep them from locking me up, Joseph. I'd have killed them because, like I say, it's easy.'

'So what's the problem, Mr Steele? Why do I get the idea that you're havin' trouble not gettin' mad at me?'

The Virginian shook his head. 'Not at you, feller. Maybe because of you. Mad at myself for allowing that bunch of homesteaders to put me in the position where the poor clods had to die.'

The half breed's puzzled anxiety expanded over several seconds and then he shrugged.

'That's too deep for me, Mr Steele.'

'Like the way I slept last night, Joseph. Which isn't usual for me. Slept with my guard down. The same way I went into the house of those crazy Harlands with my guard down. Relied on you to take care of any trouble that came up. Hell, did I say the Harland women were crazy?'

Mitchell grinned broadly. 'That's the way I want it to be, Mr Steele,' he blurted excitedly. 'And it half worked at the women's place and worked real well last night.' He saw that the Virginian's profile remained hard set and he shrugged again, the grin gone from his own features. Said in a dull tone of voice:

'Though I guess I can see your point of view. Your kind ain't used to being took care of.'

'Right, Joseph.'

'So you got to have a lot of trust in a man to allow yourself to – '

'You want to tell me about last night, feller?'

He nodded eagerly, but did not allow himself to become excited again.

'There's somethin' about the night, Mr Steele. I always feel more of an Apache at night. Maybe because it's mostly only ever at nights that I'm on my own. And I can work at being an Apache. A breed livin' with whites, he mostly has to do things the white way when the whites are all around him.

'Anyway, last night I was sharin' a camp with you, but you ain't like the whites I usually have dealin's with. So I slept like an Apache. And if you figure you're a light sleeper when you need to be, you got no idea how a fightin' Indian can sleep when he has to. Like an animal.'

114

The Virginian shot a surreptitious glance at Joseph Mitchell, and saw that the pride sounding in his voice was also visible in his Indian featured face. He looked every one of his more than fifty years now and it was difficult to visualise him in the attitude of a naive and hurt child.

'I heard riders while they was still more than a mile off, Mr Steele. And knew there were four of them. Comin' from the south. Not on the trail, though. West of the trail. Our fire was long out by then and the camp was merged in with the timber so they didn't know we was there by the pool. But they started to turn to come toward the camp. And I went out to meet them,'

'You just walked out to meet them?'

For perhaps a second now, the half breed grinned in embarrassment. Then shrugged as he answered:

'I know that wasn't Apache style, Mr Steele. But if there was gonna be trouble, I wanted to be sure you wouldn't have no chance to keep me outta it while I was figurin' on doin' the same for you.'

'Something about them made you think they were trouble, feller?'

'Aw shit, no. Except that since we met up, we ain't come across nobody who wasn't bent on trouble, Mr Steele.' Another shrug, before he went on: 'Anyway, they reined in their mounts when they saw me. And the woman started in to bad mouth me as soon as she saw I had Indian in me. Thought I was all Indian. Was as drunk as a skunk. Could smell liquor on her breath from twenty feet away. Couple of the men tried to calm her down and the other one asked me all kindsa questions about what I was doin' around this part of the country.

'Aimed the Springfield rifle at him and told the whole lot of them to be on their way. Give me a lot of pleasure to do that. Only somebody who's had to take shit most of his life could ever understand how much pleasure, Mr Steele.'

'And they went on their way, feller?'

'Not right off they didn't. Said they wanted to water their horses at the pool by the timber. I told them I wasn't gonna allow that on account of I had a sick friend sleepin' over there and he wasn't gonna be woke up. Then they said they'd go, but they'd be back through later and sick friend or not, if they wanted to water their mounts, they'd water them. And one of them said he was a deputy sheriff for this county we're in. Which was supposed to scare me, I guess. But I was the opposite of scared, Mr Steele. Especially when the woman told the men to forget about me. That they were wastin' time when they could be ridin' for the party at the Harland place.

'They went on their way then, but I knew they'd come back after they seen what happened to them two women. Knew that their minds would go straight to the Indian they had a brush with.

'And I was ready, Mr Steele.'

The Virginian glanced again at the profile of the man riding beside him. And the half breed was totally oblivious to the fact that his firmly fixed expression of proud satisfaction was under surveillance – for his mind had slipped back from this brightly sunlit morning to the darkness of the early hours.

'I knew they were comin' when they were still a long way outta sight. And I fixed up things around the camp just like I didn't know anythin' about them four bein' out there. Built the fire and lit it, got breakfast and coffee ready and set them to heat up. Then went and hid, Mr Steele. But not in the place they'd expect me to be hid. Not in the timber. I got myself out of sight in a patch of brush a half mile away. On the far side of that dip where the horses was.

'And they made it real easy for me, Mr Steele. Circled around to that side and rode down into the dip. Dismounted and went up toward the camp. Just at sunrise. Figured they was bein' real smart. But real dumb is what they was. Shit, the old timer didn't even take his rifle with him.'

Mitchell reached forward and down to caress the stock of the Winchester rifle that had replaced the single shot Springfield in the boot.

'You could have gunned them all down then, feller?'

'Uh?' the half breed grunted, jerked out of his reverie. He snatched his hand back from the repeater, like he felt it was a crime to be seen touching it.

'But my neck wasn't out far enough?'

Mitchell tried to smile, but drew no response from the stoic faced Virginian and shrugged.

'Maybe. Yeah, I figure I could have got from the brush to the horses without any of them turnin' around and spottin' me. And I could've got the old timer's Winchester outta its boot and blasted a bullet into each of them. But that wouldn't have been what I wanted, Mr Steele. So I let them four get up into the camp and then I went down among them horses soon as I heard the man wake you up. And the idea was to get the repeater and blast the two with their repeaters. Take care of the other two then. But next thing I knew, the woman was makin' tracks to come back down into the dip. With the old timer right behind her.

'That was a bad moment, I can tell you, Mr Steele. Knew that if I opened up at them, there was a good chance the men coverin' you'd start blastin'. Just had the horses for cover, and I used them. Hung on between two of the critters, fingers in the bridles and friggin' toes through riggin' rings. And prayed them two horses stayed close. They did. And they stayed sideways on to them two people comin' down the slope.

'Dumbstruck they was, when they seen me drop down from between the horses. Under the belly of one of them. Which is the way I went at them. Bare handed, Mr Steele.'

He released his hold on the reins and held up his hands, fingers clawed and wrists bent outwards.

'Came out from under the belly of that horse and sprung up at them people quicker than a mountain lion. Got a hand to each throat and had them flat on their backs before they could so much as open their mouths, let alone yell out to their buddies. And I held them down there, floppin' about like fish outta the water for awhile. Not for long though. Pretty soon they couldn't even keep a hold on me while they was tryin' to drag me off. Then they was dead from bein' strangled.

'Course, one was a woman and the other was an old timer. So I ain't claimin' much for finishin' them once I had them. But the way I got them . . .'

He looked to Steele for a comment and allowed the sentence to hang in the hot, still air.

'You're a quick thinker, Joseph. You have a particular reason for taking off their heads?'

'You saw how the men with the rifles were shaken up so bad, Mr Steele. And I had to have them that way, because I couldn't know you had them covered. Had to figure it was the one rifle against two. So I used my knife on them bodies. Cut the kind of piece of brush I needed and went up to the camp. And that's the whole thing, Mr Steele. Far as I'm concerned, I never let your neck get so far out it was in any real danger. Real glad you trusted me enough not to know about anythin' that was goin' on until them homesteaders figured they had you in a trap. And if anythin' about any of this makes you mad at anythin' or anybody, then I'm sorry. But I gotta say I'm feelin' real good to have got back some self respect. First grade or not.'

Steele nodded. 'If a man doesn't have respect for himself nothing else is worth a wooden nickel, feller.'

'But?'

The Virginian raised a gloved hand, extended the thumb and jerked it over his shoulder

'If you were a mountain lion back there, Joseph, I was a goat. And those four homesteaders were innocent bystanders who got caught up in the hunt with the tables turned. You ever use me for bait again, feller, I'll have to consider my self respect. Which will mean I won't give you any consideration.'

The half breed wore his contrite small boy expression as he listened to the cold, evenly pitched voice of Adam Steele.

'I said I was sorry if anythin' made you mad, Mr Steele,' he complained.

'And the apology's accepted, feller. It won't be a second time.'

'You want me to ride way behind you like I did at the start?'

'It's not you that smells bad, feller,' the Virginian answered evenly. 'Just that some of your ideas stink to high heaven. Don't pull any more plays like that one back there and maybe you'll live long enough to pay this debt you reckon you owe me.'

'That's crazy, Mr Steele.'

'What is, Joseph?'

'If I save your hide again, and I don't do it accordin' to your rules, then you say you'll kill me for it.'

Steele spat to the side, reflected on the point for a few moments and then nodded as he said:

'Reckon that is pretty crazy, feller. But then that's what this whole thing has been since I set you to running scared across that beach and I got a jolt of my own when I saw my double floating in the ocean.'

'The Apache in me is still scared, Mr Steele,' the half breed admitted. 'In a superstitious way, I mean. And I guess the white in me could be scared of you carryin' out the threats you been makin'. But if the chips are ever down that way, it'll be the Indian you'll be up against. And he won't owe you a thing anymore. Except a whole lot of bad because you're a white.'

This time Steele nodded, but did not spit.

'As a half Apache, I hate like hell to owe a white man even the smallest – '

'Joseph.'

'Uh?'

'I reckon you should stop thinking of yourself as a

half breed all the time.'

'It's what I am!'

'But if you lay off torturing yourself about it all the time, maybe you won't get so many half assed ideas that set you off half cocked.'

Now the Indian featured face became fixed in the expression of a small boy filled with frustration of an embittered anger he knew he dare not vent.

'You think it's easy for a man who's been treated like shit all his life to –'

'Maybe it would be better if you rode drag, feller,' Steele cut in on him.

'Be a damn pleasure, mister!'

Mitchell checked his horse and tugged on the reins to head in a new direction.

'Two fellers who prefer their own company are bound to get on each other's nerves in a situation where –'

Adam Steele had not reined in the mare and he looked impassively back over his shoulder at the half breed as the gap betweeen them got wider.

'The situation'll change!' Mitchell growled sourly to curtail the Virginian's explanation. 'And I'm sure lookin' forward to what happens when my debt's all paid.'

Steele pursed his lips and drawled softly: 'Reckon I'm not disinterested in that, Joseph.'

CHAPTER ELEVEN

THE Virginian looked back over his shoulder a great deal during the rest of the day. Both when he was in the saddle and while he rested the mare or called a halt to eat.

Sometimes he saw Joseph Mitchell – glimpsed briefly or in full view for several minutes at a time – at distances varying between a few hundred yards and more than a mile. The half breed's position as escort rider depending upon the terrain. Furthest away in totally open country. Close in when the surroundings were rugged with rock outcrops or scattered with stands of timber.

Then darkness descended upon northern California and for all he saw and heard, Adam Steele might well have been the only man in this area of the western foothills of the Coast Range of mountains. Which was exactly the impression he expected to have in relation to the half breed. Who would have moved up close after the sun set: but taken great pains to remain unseen in the light of the moon and unheard in the shadowy rises and hollows of this hill country.

Hidden to the eyes of the Virginian and silent to his ears. Quite simply as a matter of pride. For there was no reason to suspect that an imminent threat to either man lurked out in the night through which they rode. And in which they then camped.

For the Six Rivers County relatives, friends and neighbours of the dead, and the vigilantes from Golden Hill, were not in the immediate vicinity of the two men. Of this fact Steele was absolutely certain and, if he chose to consider it, was sure that Joseph Mitchell shared his conviction.

During the long ride through the hot day into the cool evening and night – on a constantly north eastern route – Steele had never been primarily concerned with whether or not the half breed was still shadowing him. He rode and rested as he normally did: apparently nonchalant but actually vigilant and alert. Trusting Joseph Mitchell, but only as an ally. Which was not how it had been yesterday and last night when, in humouring the man he had allowed himself to be lulled into a false sense of security. But yesterday and last night had been different.

With Vic Judd and Ryan King permanently out of contention for the stolen gold and no sign that the other grubbers from Golden Hill were still on the trail of the wrong man, it had seemed safe to rely on the half breed to ride herd on him. While he struggled to come to terms with an image which seemed certain to remain seared into the forefront of his mind for all time – of himself, sodden and inert at the edge of the ocean with a bullet in his back.

The brush with death at the Harland homestead should have warned Steele to recall the lessons of the past. One lesson in particular. That it was foolish – sometimes even dangerously stupid – to dwell on any wrong in the past that could not be righted in the present or future. But he ignored the warning at the crude shack of the crazy women.

With good reason? Emma and Joan Harland caused their deadly trouble in isolation. Totally unrelated to violence that had triggered a chain reaction from a town called Golden Hill.

No, that was not a good reason at all. Not for Adam Steele who knew from countless experiences in the past that the present and the future were destined to explode at any waking or sleeping moment a fresh threat to his life. And that his life was always in greatest danger when he allowed his guard to drop – invariably in the most apparently innocuous surroundings.

Thus had he slept like a drugged man at last night's camp – perhaps deep in his subconscious still concerned at seemingly coming face to face with his own corpse – without for a moment considering the obvious dangers.

That for the first time in many weeks he was bedded down in a settled area of country.

That after taking a hand in the killing of two settlers he had followed the trail that connected their outlying homestead with those of neighbours.

That some of those neighbours might just do what some of them did and go visit with the Harland mother and daughter.

That Joseph Mitchell, the half breed with an enormous chip on his shoulder, would have an opportunity to take advantage of being humoured. To discharge half his debt before the Virginian could repeat what happened at the Harland homestead, take a hand in his own defence and so diminish the part played by Mitchell.

Bedded down now at the mouth of a narrow ravine with twenty feet high rock walls, Adam Steele was very much a man chastened by experience: firmly convinced that there were some mistakes he would never make again. A shallow brand of sleep that was nonetheless restful came easily to him as he lay under a blanket and the sheepskin coat, his head on the pillow of his saddle and his hat over his face. A gloved hand fisted around the frame of the Colt Hartford. His mind primed to be instantly aware of nearby danger and his muscles ready to respond with whatever action he commanded of them. This irrespective of what the embittered half breed would do.

'Hello, Joseph,' Steele said as soon as he cracked open his eyes to the half light under his hat.

'I been here a whole hour at least, mister.'

'But you don't intend me any harm until after you've stopped somebody else from killing me.'

Steele wriggled into a seated posture on his saddle and tipped the Stetson off his face and on to his head. Yawned and rasped the back of a hand across the bristles on his jaw as he looked up at the half breed. Who stood just beyond the narrow mouth of the ravine, against a backdrop of grey sky that perhaps augured rain. For the moment, though, the dawn air was chill but not damp.

'Ain't stayin', mister.'

It was very strange the way the Indian features of this middle aged half breed could appear so youthful despite the heavy growth of black beard on the lower half. And the more broodingly sullen he was, the more the years appeared to disappear: like he was wearing some kind of mask through which it was just possible to glimpse his true identity.

'And I reckon you didn't stop by to get breakfast again, Joseph?'

'Damn right. Come to tell you that I ain't fooled, mister.'

'I tried to fool you?'

'Maybe. But if you did, I ain't. The way you rode all through yesterday – and the way I guess you'll go today . . . ' He waved toward the north east. 'It's toward Golden Hill.'

'I never was there, feller. And with no trail to follow, I could be way off line. Reach a point where we'll start to get further away instead of closer. Be grateful if you'll steer me right when I start to go wrong.'

'Why are you headin' for Golden Hill, mister?'

'It's in a direct line away from a place where some people are sure to be looking for some other people, feller. And when they find them, they'll start looking for me. Maybe already have found them and are already looking for me.'

'I told you before I ain't so dumb,' Mitchell said dully as he watched Steele get out of his bedroll, don the sheepskin coat and furl the blankets. 'I knew we couldn't go south. That folks down that way'd be sure to see us. And remember us after the dead was found – a soft talkin' dude and a dirty half breed. But there was lotsa other ways we could've gone. You come this way and I just want you to know that I know Golden Hill's over in them mountains, mister.'

He waved again in the same direction as before, toward an area of the Coast Range Steele was unable to see from within the mouth of the ravine. And then he spun on his bare heels and set off at a run. Within moments was out of sight on the downslope which fell away from the ravine.

And Steele did not look in his wake until after he

127

had saddled the chestnut mare and lashed his bedroll into place. Led the horse out from between the high walls. When he made a sweeping survey of the entire expanse of terrain spread out to the south west. And failed to see the half breed, who might have been concealed in one of at least a hundred patches of cover large enough to hide a man and a horse. But he did see a large body of riders at least ten miles away. This possible because of the height of his vantage point, the clearness of the air unhazed by heat shimmer and the flatness of the verdant plain beyond the foothills.

The Virginian watched the distant group for a few seconds and saw they were making fast time over ground which would have retained signs easy for a skilled tracker to follow. Then he shortened the focus of his eyes, but not to seek out the hiding place of Joseph Mitchell. Instead, to search for any clues the half breed may have left to ease the difficulties of the followers in tracking two men over the less lush, far more rocky terrain of the foothills. But there was nothing to be seen over such a distance and Steele swung astride the mare and resumed his ride toward the high ridges in back of the foothills. Prepared to give Mitchell the benefit of the doubt for now. But keeping an open mind about what the half breed was likely to do if the Six Rivers County people decided to split into smaller groups when they came into the hills.

He estimated there were something between twenty and thirty men in the group crossing the flatlands. Which was surely too many even for a part Apache flexing his newly discovered' arrogance in dealing with the despised whites. But four or five or even six . . . Joseph Mitchell would reckon to take care of such a small bunch of homesteaders who were angry and sickened by what happened to their friends and neighbours – but unskilled in hunting and killing anything outside of game.

Steele was sure the pursuers had not seen him as a lone rider against the backdrop of many-coloured hills. But he waited until intervening high ground reared up behind him before he asked for a gallop from the mare – so that there was no chance of the kicked up billows of dust being spotted from far to the south west.

Now he no longer made direct progress in his chosen direction. Instead veered from left to right – somtimes veering very wide to one or other side. Not so much to confuse the followers as to avoid being skylined on hill crests and thus giving the men behind him a clear bearing.

He did not expect to shake off Joseph Mitchell and sometimes saw, less often heard, but mostly merely sensed the presence of the half breed in back of him.

Until the rain came.

Came first as a cold and sodden mist sweeping down from the tree clad slopes of the mountains. To spook the mare and disorientate the man: to such an extent that he reined in the horse and dismounted. Remained where he was under a treetopped bluff after he had draped a slicker over his shoulders. Knowing, with his back against the water darkened rock of the cliff face that Mitchell – when his gelding last snorted – had been maybe three hundred yards away to the right.

Now, in addition to reducing visibility to virtually zero, the heavy mist also acted to deaden sound.

And played tricks with a man's physical senses to such a degree that he would be a fool to trust that which is known as the sixth.

Then the mist ceased to slide past down the slope and for several seconds was chillingly unmoving. And between the intake and expellation sounds of the Virginian and the horse breathing, the dripping of water from tree boughs seemed to be amplified out of all proportion to reality. Which for several moments caused Steele – not normally given to allowing his imagination free rein – to see in his mind's eye the two blood spilling heads on the cleft stick held aloft by the half breed.

But the teeming rain that deluged from the clouds above the treetops was too intense to be heard as anything except a monotone hiss that was reminiscent of nothing save other downpours. And now Steele could see several yards ahead as he ran a gloved hand over the neck of the mare to calm her. Could still not see nor hear nor sense if the half breed had remained where he was when the mist first enveloped this area of the mountains.

At least, though, he knew the pursuers from the homesteading valley were still more miles away than when he saw them just after daybreak. And Joseph Mitchell would not pose a threat to him unless and until they closed the large gap. Which he now sought to maintain if not to widen – by pushing on through the storm which could well cause the men from Six Rivers County to call a halt.

He covered about a half mile, leading the mare by the bridle, and keeping close to the bluff which he had seen ran more due east than north east just before the mist came down. And there he took shelter under a slight overhang of rock, chewed on some jerked beef and stamped his booted feet to keep the circulation going while he grimaced at the storm. Protected from the vertically falling rain, but stamping in several rivulets that coursed over the sloping, rocky ground. Able to see a lone pine from time to time that he knew was a marker to the direction he wanted to go. But not so sure if he would be able to get a new bearing from this point. And preferring the scant shelter of the jutting rock face to the leaking cover of a pine tree on the exposed crest of a slope.

It was difficult to judge the passing of time, for the discomforts of being out in the chilling deluge acted to stretch the usual measurements. Which was not a fresh experience for Adam Steele, who had endured worse weather than this on many occasions in the past. And knew that all a man could do was guard against the dangers of exposure, curb his impatience to be moving on, not allow his imagination to dominate his powers of rational thinking, and wait for the worst to be over.

'Aw shit, mister!' the half breed yelled from about thirty yards away to Steele's left. 'You gonna spend the whole damn day under that rock makin' waves in them pools?'

The Virginian allowed himself just a short, tight grin of satisfaction as he continued to stamp his feet. And folded his arms so that his gloved hands were locked under his armpits. This as he watched Mitchell ride toward him – still barefoot and bareheaded but with a poncho formed of a blanket with a slit cut in it to drape his shoulders.

'The white half of you getting the upper hand,

Joseph?' Steele asked as the rider halted his horse just a few feet outside of the shelter of the rock.

'I ain't gonna deny I'm friggin' cold and gettin' colder out in the open, mister. Same as you ain't exactly glowin' warm where you are. So it's best for both of us if we keep movin', I guess.'

'I'm a stranger here, Joseph.'

'I ain't, mister. From here I know the way to where we're headed. And if you're ready to forget for awhile this crazy thing we got between us, I'll be glad to lead you.'

He raised his cupped hands to his mouth, breathed hard into them and pressed them to his cheeks. Rubbed one over the tip of his nose. Which was darkly purple in colour.

'Reckon the war's been over long enough, feller,' Steele called against the hiss of the falling rain. This as he unfolded his arms and moved alongside the mare to slide his booted left foot into the stirrup.

'War?'

'The Stars and Bars was my flag back then, feller,' the Virginian answered as he settled in the saddle. 'But I reckon I'm now about ready to follow the red, white and blue.'

CHAPTER TWELVE

THE two men rode through the constant deluge of cold mountain rain in line astern, with never more than a half dozen feet separating the leading gelding from the following mare.

While Joseph Mitchell went to a great deal of trouble to try to deceive Adam Steele. Did not assume that the Virginian trusted him as implicitly as he had seemed to at the outset and so led him along a tortuous route of twists and turns through the foothills and on the mountainside while the rain continued to sheet out of the low sky.

This smokescreen of ever changing directions in limited visibility designed to leave Steele completely disorientated. Unaware that instead of gradually moving up and into the Coast Range on an obstacle littered north easterly line, the half breed was in fact either backtracking to the west or half circling and then reversing the arc of travel so that the two men reached more or less the same starting points after several minutes of slow riding.

Once, after the charade had been in progress for upwards of half an hour during which neither man had spoken, the Virginian asked:

'We're still a long way from Golden Hill, I reckon?'

'We sure are, Mr Steele,' came the eager reply, Mitchell using the courtesy title plus the surname for the first time in a long time.

'How far, feller?'

'With luck, we could be there by midday tomorrow.'

'Joseph?'

'Yeah, Mr Steele?'

'How come a dogsbody in a cathouse knows the country such a long way from home so well, Joseph?'

The half breed had always known without needing to look that the Virginian was close behind him. So it was now for the first time since they started away from the bluff that he snapped his head around to peer through the teeming rain at Steele. And discovered the man was eyeing him with an expression that appeared to be of genuine interest, unsullied by mistrust.

'I had time off sometimes,' Mitchell answered as he faced front again. 'July four and Christmas and some weeks Sundays. Often as not on them days, Miss Sophie'd let me have the loan of a horse. And I'd take off on my own outta Golden Hill. Cover the country on all sides of that town. Made it my territory, sort of. Apache style, sort of.'

'Just know every blade of grass and piece of rock on it, uh Joseph? Without understanding why or how?'

'That's right, Mr Steele.'

They were starting up a slope and the Virginian, his tongue very firmly in his cheek, suggested:

'I know what you mean, feller. You could no more say what's over this hill than I could. But you just know we're heading in the right direction.'

'That's right, Mr Steele. That's exactly right. You've had dealin's with Indians before, I figure.'

'A time or two, Joseph.'

Talk was done with then. Steele remaining silent because he did not want to tip his hand by overplaying the part of the innocent. And Mitchell kept quiet, the Virginian guessed, because he needed to concentrate his entire attention on not getting lost – while at the same time varying the route sufficiently to guard against the following rider seeing through the trick.

Probably, too, Steele thought, the half breed offered up a plea to the god or spirit of his choice each time he tilted his head to peer skywards – requesting that the rain keep falling as heavily as ever until it had served his purpose

And it pleased whatever deity he called upon to grant his request.

For more than two hours and perhaps long into the third – being uncomfortably encapsuled in a severely restricted world of cold and wet and near silence continued to distort the Virginian's reckoning of the passage of time – the rain teemed upon the land. Turning soft ground into quagmires and forming minor torrents of rushing water on the rockier downslopes. Beating at riders and horses as though in a concerted and premeditated attempt to break their spirits.

And the gelding and the mare were certainly morosely despondent in obeying the commands of the riders. Experiencing the worst of it by having to wade through mud and water as well as enduring the relentless assault of the falling rain – while perhaps knowing in their equine brains that much of the ground they were covering had been gone over before.

Adam Steele shook his head at this and vented a just audible snarl of self anger. If horses thought at all beyond the need to perform natural functions, it was simply in relation to doing what was asked of them. If a turn was commanded, it would be made. But if the horse knew it was moving back and forth over the same stretch of ground time and time again, it would do so automatically until the rider issued a new command.

The Virginian rasped a louder sound and the half breed turned just his head to ask evenly:

'You say somethin', Mr Steele?'

It seemed like a long time to the Virginian but in retrospect he decided it must have only taken him a second or so to win the struggle against the impulse to unleash his anger at the weather battered but serenely calm Joseph Mitchell. And reply:

'Just to my horse, feller. Said I hope they have a livery at Golden Hill where she can get a rub down and rest up in a dry stall.'

'They got one.'

The half breed faced front again, riding rigidly erect in the saddle: unbowed by the rain that pasted his hair to his head and kept the sodden blanket become poncho plastered to his torso like a thick outer skin.

And the Virginian made the effort to sit erect in his saddle and to unhunch his shoulders under the slicker that at least kept his upper body dry. Despite his earlier periods of introspection, he had allowed his guard to drop again. He had set out to let the damn half breed think he was being fooled – with the resolute intention of teaching the crazy sonofabitch a lesson – but then found he was falling into the trap.

He knew Joseph Mitchell was leading him away from Golden Hill. And, more than this, was hoping to get him close enough to the Six Rivers County people to stage another murderous rescue.

But it was taking too long, in conditions that remained constantly bad. To the extent that Steele began to have doubts about his own motives, at a point when he felt he had invested too much time, effort and discomfort to abandon what he was doing. And to keep from dwelling on this, had forced himself to consider other aspects of this crazy, zig-zagging and half circling, backtracking and returning ride in a rainstorm. Which had caused him to lose his concentration – to the extent that he became as dejected as his horse and even sought to sympathise with the animal by trying to guess what she was thinking.

While all this time an older man, whose most recent line of work was fetching and carrying for the whores in a mining town cathouse, remained sharply alert to his surroundings and totally in control of his responses to whatever was happening in those surroundings.

Yet again the Virginian felt an impulse to self anger, but on this occasion did not vent any sound. Simply shook his head violently, spraying water outwards from the brim of his Stetson. Disgusted with himself now for the way he was thinking of Joseph Mitchell – who was no more of a crazy sonofabitch for acting the way he did than was Adam Steele for going along with it. And it mattered not at all that circumstances had led to the half breed doing menial work in a whorehouse.

A man did what he had to in order to survive.

All this silently admitted during the part of a second it took for the Virginian's head to move from one side to another – while his eyes remained fixed on a single point to the right of the ramrod stiff form of Mitchell riding slowly some six feet in front of him.

A point where, a few seconds earlier, he might well have merely thought he saw a man. But where now – his mind shaken clear of all that was superfluous – he knew he had seen one. Appeared and disappeared in almost the blinking of an eye as he rode at an angle across the path of the half breed and the Virginian. Seen purely by chance by Steele who happened to have moved his head to the right: and missed by Mitchell who at that moment ducked his head to rub the rain from an eye with the back of a hand.

Steele jerked a hand to the stock of the Colt Hartford as he continued to peer ahead to the right where there was now just a slick wall of teeming rain. Identical to that which showed on the periphery of his vision.

And he now looked to the other side of the stiffly riding, obviously unsuspecting half breed. Into another wall of rain.

So had the momentarily seen rider been alone, having converged on the path being ridden by Mitchell and Steele: to cross it some thirty feet in front of the half breed? Unaware of the presence of other men so close? Or was he the backmarker of a string of riders? Any number from a handful up to the perhaps thirty or so Steele had seen from the vantage point of the ravine mouth early this morning?

But whatever the situation beyond the encircling

rain wall, the immediate danger was gone. The half breed had not seen the stranger and the stranger had failed to realise there was anybody in back of him.

But Steele was not prepared to let it rest there. He still had a gloved hand on the stock of the Colt Hartford and now he took a grip around the frame of the rifle – and slid it smoothly out of the boot. Thumbed back the hammer and aimed the barrel alongside the neck of the mare, one handed, to draw a bead on the back of the half breed.

Yelled: 'Here's the bastard that killed them! I got a rifle on him!'

Joseph Mitchell reined his gelding to a halt and wrenched his head around. A look of fear, hatred and despair contorting his Indian featured face.

While off to the right the voices of several men were raised to shout questions.

But the half breed's words sounded clearly against the other voices and the hiss of rain when he challenged:

'So friggin' shoot, why don't you?'

And then he was facing front again. His bare heels thudded into the flanks of his horse and he wrenched on the reins – to wheel the gelding away from the chorus of excited voices and plunge him into a gallop. Racing blindly through the constantly yielding wall of rain which might well be concealing a whole range of palpably dangerous obstacles to bring horse and rider crashing down at virtually every step.

Steele tracked the rifle to within a foot of keeping the turning man covered. And squeezed the trigger just before he disappeared through the rain – the bullet thus cracking far wide of what had never been a target anyway.

'Shit!' he snarled in the immediate wake of the gunshot.

The expletive heard by three riders who loomed out of the rain to the right of where Steele sat his mare, the Colt Hartford stock pressed into his shoulder as he continued to aim in the wrong direction.

'What the hell's happenin' here?'

'Who the frig are you?'

'Damnit, let's get after him!'

All three men snarled at the same time and two others emerged from the wall of rain to join them: as Steele punctuated what they said with a second shot.

'Come on then!' somebody snapped.

And commanded his mount to lunge in the direction the Virginian had fired. Two more followed him, one of them shrieking over his shoulder:

'No more shootin', mister! You could hit one of us!'

Then these three had ridden from sight into the rain, clawing revolvers or rifles out from under their all-engulfing slickers.

'I said who the frig are you?' one of the two strangers who had not joined the chase demanded.

'Nobody you'd know, feller,' Steele drawled evenly as he turned his head slowly to look at the two slicker draped men who were craned slightly forward in their saddles – to survey him as intently as possible without moving their mounts closer.

One of them mistrusting him while the other merely looked scared. The first in his sixties and the second about twenty. One heavily bearded and the other looking like he perhaps had not yet started to shave. Both of them tall and thin.

'So how come you know we're lookin' for a killer?'

'Two killers, Gramps!'

'Speak when you're spoke to, boy!'

Steele had the stock of the rifle to his shoulder still and was looking over it and the wrist of his right hand at the men, who had their hands out of sight under their slickers.

'Could tell you I ran into some more people like you and they told me all about it, feller.'

'But that would be a lie and I'd know it, son,' the mistrustful older man with the beard growled. 'See, me and the boy here and them three you sent off on the wild goose chase was all that pressed on when the rain started. Rest turned for home.'

'Gramps, I don't get none of this!'

'Somethin' called divide and conquer, boy. This is one of them that killed your Pa and the Widow Perry, Weeks and Phil Tucker and the Harland women. Other one's drawn off –'

'Like for you to take off after your friends and neighbours, Mr Jackson,' Steele interrupted, the Colt Hartford still aimed away from the two Six Rivers County people. 'So that maybe there doesn't have to be any more killing.'

'Just maybe, son?' the bearded man posed dully while the young one kept switching his attention between his grandfather and the Virginian.

'You and your friends and neighbours plan on getting me to the town of Fort Trinity so I can be tried for murder, Mr Jackson. The feller I'm riding with is dead set on keeping that from happening. Unless you give up the chase, I can't promise you safe passage back to where you came from. The valley . . . isn't that what you people call it?'

'That's what we call the piece of land where we live sure enough. And it's a fine place for a man to put down roots and raise a family. But I figure it'll be a livin' hell for me if I go back there knowin' I let the murderer of my son just walk away free from me.'

He was hampered by age and the rain and the all-enveloping slicker. His moves in drawing the revolver from its holster as slow as his talk. But, inevitably, the gun was clear of the holster and then came out from under the slicker. To draw a bead on Steele, even though he had raked the Colt Hartford around to aim it at the old man's chest.

'Gramps!' the young man shrieked and wrenched his head around to shrill in the same tone at the Virginian: 'Please don't, mister!'

Emotion rather than conditions played tricks with time now. And it seemed that for a very long time the old man was on the brink of being blasted to violent death while Adam Steele endured agonies of indecision. And the potential victim of the lethal rifle in his rock steady grip became increasingly certain of what he had to do. But it could not have lasted for more than three seconds.

When Steele triggered a shot a part of the next second before the revolver in the wavering grip of the old man would have been aimed at him. While the young man was still in process of sliding a rifle out of the boot to back the suicidal play of his grandfather.

A shot that served its purpose to some extent. Acted to freeze the young man in his moves to swing the Winchester to the aim while he pumped the lever action of the rifle – with his head wrenched to the side to see what happened to his grandfather.

But a shot that had absolutely no effect on the old man. Who perhaps was not even aware of a tug on the chinstrap as the deliberately aimed bullet tunnelled a hole into the front and then out the back of his hat.

'Scum!' the unshocked bearded man said coldly as the gun in his hand came to the aim and he squeezed the trigger.

Steele bared his teeth and rasped. 'Crazy's right.'

This as the bullet cracked out through the muzzle flash of the sixshooter in the old man's hand and bit deep into his flesh. Spun him part way around in the saddle with its impact. So that he had to cling tight with his legs to stay on the mare.

'Feller has to be a half-wit to get a hole this way.'

CHAPTER THIRTEEN

THE chestnut mare was schooled to gunfire and so was undisturbed by the dual crack of a revolver and a rifle. Was schooled, also, to obey immediately the commands of her rider. And was familiar enough with his touch to recognise when a greater or lesser degree of a normal action was called for. Thus instinctively responded to the thud of unspurred heels against her flanks – lunged into an instant gallop. To carry the grimacing Virginian at high speed away from the old and the young men as they struggled to bring under control their mounts which were not at all used to close quarters gunfire.

Adam Steele's initial impulse was to regain firm control over the mare after the animal had misinterpreted the reason for his heeling action. And he reached for and clung to the reins – while he still gripped the Colt Hartford – with the intention of doing this.

But then he heard shouting through the teeming rain behind him. And shots. Became aware of a sticky warmth on his flesh in the area of his upper right chest. Abruptly experienced the weakening effect of shock as his mind registered to the exclusion of all else that he had been shot.

For the first time in a life largely spent on the borderline between living and dying by the gun, somebody had put a bullet into him.

He stayed clinging to the rifle and to the reins with his gloved hands and to the sides of the mare with his knees and feet. His body canted forward very low, so that his left cheek was almost against the neck of the horse. The kind of way he would have elected to ride had he been aware of bullets cracking after him. The horse galloping at the kind of head long pace he would have demanded had he known a bunch of men who wanted him dead were hot on his trail. But watching where the horse was carrying him at such speed. Straining his cracked open eyes to peer through the wall of rain – intent upon steering the mare clear of natural obstacles that might tumble and kill him: or leave him helplessly unable to defend himself when the pursuers came for him.

But the knowledge that he had a bullet buried in his flesh rendered him incapable of consciously considering any other threat to his well-being – and that was not supposed to happen. By the rules he had always played this violent game of life, it was the other people who got shot. He would suffer a little pain occasionally, but he should not have to endure a bullet wound. Especially not out in wild mountain country a lot of miles from the nearest doctor. Where he might well die: a long and lingering death.

Hell, the sonsofbitches had stripped him emotionally – made it so that he was not even able to feel a pang of disappointment when he lost everything that made life worthwhile for ordinary men. Now they were going to force him to endure physical agony.

The shooting and the shouting by the five men from the homesteaders' valley of Six Rivers County did not last for long. The gallop of the chestnut mare went on for a great deal longer. The rain did not slacken until mid-day nor stop until an hour later. The homesteaders were on their way back home by then, knowing they had lost one of the two killers and hoping that the bullet drilled into the other one would prove fatal. The horse had run until exhausted, then staggered and rolled and lay on her side in a thicket of brush under the brow of a low hill. Five miles from where the blind run through the rainstorm began. And Adam Steele was thrown from her back as the mare fell. Turned twice in the air and wondered if this was the sensation of dying. Then thudded to the rain sodden ground. Opened his mouth to vent a cry of agony as the impact exploded excruciating pain out of mere soreness, then became gripped by unfeeling unconsciousness. Was spread-eagled on his back, his mouth involuntarily closed against the beat of the rain: while his right hand opened, to release his hold on the Colt Hartford. But the rifle remained lying across the palm.

Of this, the Virginian knew nothing. And was only intermittently aware of what happened during the rest of that day and the two days and nights that followed. When, in the grey light of dawn, a man growled:

'What're you doin' back here, you dirty double dealin' killer?'

A woman said shrilly: 'He's shot!'

'But he ain't dead yet!'

'You figure there's enough life left in him to string him up?'

Adam Steele had been riding for maybe an hour with his eyes squeezed tightly closed and his chin resting down on his chest. Needed to use a lot of effort to bring up his head: less to open his eyes to the morning light.

'Man, you're a friggin' mess, Ethan Winston!' somebody in the large crowd of people clustered around the weary mare and sick rider snarled.

And there was a chorus of murmuring agreement with this, the underlying tone of all of it carrying a rasp of animosity.

The Virginian saw them and their town as a blur. Struggled to recall why it was so important to him to be here. When the voices had quietened down started to say:

'If you people want to see a worse mess . . .'

A man demanded to know: 'What's the sonofa-bitch sayin'? He drunk or somethin'?'

'Weak from gettin' shot and losin' his blood, I figure,' the man who clasped the bridle of the mare answered. 'What's that you're sayin', Winston?'

Steele made an effort to raise his voice as he shifted his head from side to side: to survey the whole crowd of perhaps twenty men and a half dozen women grouped to either side and in front of his horse. Tried to bring them and the town beyond them into sharp focus.

'I said if you . . . want to see . . . a worse mess . . . you should look . . . underneath what's on the . . . outside.'

'Skunk through and through and head to toe, Ethan Winston.'

The Virginian sucked in a deep breath of air, intent upon replying loud and clear that he was not who they thought he was. But his nostrils filled with the pungent stink of himself and he came close to gagging. On a stench of stale sweat and other body

148

wastes and, worst of all, the sweet smell of gangrene. Squeezed his eyes closed on the unclear scene and managed to rasp out through gritted teeth before physical pain transcended and swamped mental anguish and he slumped from the saddle:

'I sure do smell that bad, feller.'

CHAPTER FOURTEEN

DAWN had broken an hour ago, but there was no sun yet. And from the look of the sky – low and a dirty grey in colour – perhaps there would be none to warm the damp chill of night before darkness fell again. But there would be no rain, either. So just a dull and gloomy day that most people who lived at Golden Hill would have to admit was a match for their loose knit, cheerless, poverty ridden community.

It was not much of a town: comprised of a short, one sided street along the crest of a broad and gentle south west facing incline. Claims, most with a shack on them but a few with just a tent or a dugout for the grubbers to live in, were spread far and wide over the slope. Connected by a network of well trodden pathways to each other and with the street on the top of the hill. Where there was Miss Sophie's Saloon, a livery stable, an assay office and bank, two stores and a bakery. All of them frame built and in a bad state of repair.

There was only one tree on the hill – an ancient oak at the north west end of the street, just beyond the final building which was the bakery. And it was toward this oak that four men carried the unconscious form of Adam Steele. While a woman led the mare by the reins and the initial crowd that had gathered to watch the lone rider enter town from the south east trail grew larger by the moment: swollen by grubbers drawn from their claims and merchants, clerks and whores from their places of business. Converging on the hanging tree to witness Ethan Winston paying for the crime of robbing and killing Dan Webb. Just as they had seen his partner in crime get hanged last week.

That had been a sunny day, when they had strung up the whore. Before the big rain storms came to sweep through the mountains. With dark smoke from near a hundred stacks rising high into the cloudless sky and the delicious aroma of baking bread a lot less pronounced than it was this morning as the large crowd of Golden Hill citizens shuffled to a halt out front of the bakery. Citizens who were as one with their town in the matter of appearance.

Only a handful of them young and the vast majority elderly. Just Miss Sophie and the whores and the man who ran the bank and assay office chose to being clean and showing a certain sense of style in their garbs. Everyone else poorly dressed in unlaundered clothing that was torn and patched, or simply torn. And mostly these people were unshaven and unwashed for many days. So most everybody smelled – individually not as bad as the Virginian, but as a crowd contributing to a stink that meant they were all insensitive to the evil scent of gangrene and much else that emanated from him.

There were two benches beneath the spreading branches of the ancient oak and men were quick and eager to follow the instructions of the white bearded old man who had, without drawing protests, taken charge of the situation: to drag the benches away from the trunk and align them side by side, with a gap of some six feet between, under a stout branch about fifteen feet above the ground.

Then the woman with the mare was told to manoeuvre the animal between the benches, when the reins were surrendered to the man with the white beard.

Next, the four men who had carried the unconscious Steele along the street undertook the more arduous and awkward chore of raising him back into his saddle and, two standing on the bench to one side of the horse and two the other, held him there – upright from rump to shoulders, but with his head slumped forward, chin on his chest again.

Which was the attitude Steele had maintained for every waking moment since he hauled himself into the saddle after recovering consciousness in the wake of the rain storm two days and nights ago. Getting weaker by the hour as the infection in his bullet wound spread through his bloodstream to start the fires of fevers in his head. Which were followed by bouts of cold sweat that left him shivering and with his teeth chattering. Always worst at the dawning of the day when he awoke on whatever patch of ground he had collapsed to when night came. Awoke to haul himself wearily back astride his horse and ride again. Feeling no pain: or tormented by pain. In whatever condition, able to keep one clear thought in a mind that was otherwise a blurred blank or was crowded with anguish – he was not going to die. Never had he been more certain of anything. And to ensure that he did not die, he had to get to a doctor who would dig out the bullet and treat the damage it had done.

There would be a doctor for the homesteaders of Six Rivers County, but he could not seek help there.

Because he was wanted for murder in the valley, and was known by sight to certain of the homesteaders. Known because he had let the crazy half breed lead him into a trap then had allowed the homesteaders who never did have the drop on him to live.

What a mess . . .

He smelled baking bread and recalled somebody telling him he was a mess. Somebody in Golden Hill. Which was the destination he had kept firmly in his mind as he rode blindly across the foothills and through the mountains that were entirely strange to him. Willing himself to head the mare in the right direction so that he would arrive at a place where there was a doctor to treat him: and where he was not wanted for murder. But he was!

'He's comin' outta it!' a man to the right of Steele announced.

'That's fine,' the man with the white beard who held the reins of the mare replied. 'You should know you're bein' hung, Ethan Winston. For the killin' of your partner Daniel Webb. You should know as well that we didn't need the breed to tell us. That Miss Sophie's new girl admitted the whole thing when we caught her sneakin' outta town to come meet up with you. So if you come back to Golden Hill for her, you sure are gonna be near her. On account of we figure to bury your carcase in the same hole, Winston. Seein' as how the dirt's fresh dug and won't be so much hard work to dig it again. You got anythin' you wanna say?'

Adam Steele had never felt weaker and sicker. He was vividly aware of everything that was being said to him but felt powerless to even speak, let alone act, to try to extricate himself from what was the most

154

dangerous situation in which he had ever been.

Then a hand reached down from above – and knocked off his hat. Took a grip on his grey hair and jerked up his head – so that a noose could be dropped around his neck.

He saw the street and the claims and the man with the white beard and the four who held him in the saddle. And the audience for his execution. All of them grim faced as they watched the noose being tightened around his neck. Then he felt hot breath against his left ear and heard a familiar voice whisper in a demanding tone:

'Can you understand what I'm sayin'?'

The Virginian's eyes moved along their sockets and rolled up. To look away from the expectant gazes of the miners and the merchants and the whores. To locate at close quarters the grinning features of Joseph Mitchell – as haggard, heavily bristled and filthy as his own.

'I can handle it from here,' the half breed told the men on the benches who were holding Steele in his saddle. And they let go of him and stepped to the ground: went to join the main body of watchers. Which divided into two groups in response to a motion by the man with the white beard – so that a gap of some ten feet was opened up in front of the old timer and the horse he was holding.

'Figure that means you can,' Mitchell whispered for Steele's benefit only, as he tightened still further the noose around the neck of the helpless man. While with his other hand he gripped the collar of the sheepskin coat and held himself in the tree with his legs wrapped around the branch. 'Want you to know I was behind you all the way here, mister.

155

Ready to haul you into town if you needed it. Or to steer you right if you looked like gettin' lost. But you never did, so this is the only way I can figure to even us up.'

'Enough of that, breed!' the man with the white beard barked, misinterpreting Mitchell's motives as a murmuring of impatience started to sound among the two groups of watchers. 'I'll not stand for you gloatin' over the fact we allowed you to take part in the execution!'

'Bastards!' the half breed hissed. Then, very fast, as he shifted his dark eyed gaze from the old man to Steele: 'It's a lousy knot up here, mister. All you gotta do is hold on to the horse and keep her runnin'. Way I held on to that branch when you was pullin' me outta the sand when –'

'I said enough, breed!' the man who held the mare snarled. And abruptly was not holding the reins any longer. Stepped from the front to the rear of the animal. And leaned across a bench to bring an open hand down on her rump.

'Good –' the Virginian blurted through teeth gritted so tight together his jaw hurt – this part of the exercise in intense concentration as he sought to regain control of the muscles in his pain ravaged body. And got his gloved hands up from his sides to grip the saddlehorn. At the same time as he raised both feet and thrust them into the stirrups. And tensed his neck and shoulders to expect the bone snapping wrench of the hanging rope as the hands of Joseph Mitchell released their grip on noose and coat collar. And felt a momentary tautness of the rope between the tree branch and the neck, when he was sure the half breed had tricked him. Was not a crazy half Apache prepared to go to extreme lengths to repay a debt of honour. Instead was just a dumb half white ready to sacrifice his hard won self respect in some faint hope of being accepted as an equal by the defeated people of this squalid town. But then the rope streaked through the running knot on the branch and Steele – briefly jerked back by the tension – went suddenly forward. And his cry of pain as the movement exploded new agony in his infected chest wound, was drowned out by the shrill screams of rage as the people of Golden Hill vented their feelings at seeing the doomed man carried away free by the runaway mare. While Joseph Mitchell half fell and half jumped to the ground, apparently attacked by a paroxysm of self anger that he had failed to secure the hanging rope. And he was one of the first to recover and start to yell to his fellow citizens to get their horses and give chase. Before he and the others of like mind were countered by the white bearded man, who pointed out that the escaper was doomed to die anyway from the bullet rotting his flesh. With which the calming crowd eventually agreed. By which time the Virginian was long gone back down the trail by which he had entered the town of Golden Hill. Clinging desperately to the saddlehorn and with his feet jammed hard in the stirrups. Once more relying almost entirely on the chestnut mare to gallop him out of danger. With neither the time nor the inclination to reflect that the speed of a snapped neck or the bite of a bullet into a vital organ might well be a fate preferable to that which awaited him out here in desolate country with the poison of infection gradually becoming more virulent in his body. Aware only that he managed to force out –

many minutes and miles too late for the half breed to hear – the conclusion of the farewell . . .

'. . . BYE.'

*

For now, until Adam Steele's story is continued in the next book of the series.

**Give them
the pleasure of choosing**

Book Tokens can be bought
and exchanged at most
bookshops in Great Britain
and Ireland.

NEL BESTSELLERS

T51277	'THE NUMBER OF THE BEAST'	*Robert Heinlein*	£2.25
T50777	STRANGER IN A STRANGE LAND	*Robert Heinlein*	£1.75
T51382	FAIR WARNING	*Simpson & Burger*	£1.75
T52478	CAPTAIN BLOOD	*Michael Blodgett*	£1.75
T50246	THE TOP OF THE HILL	*Irwin Shaw*	£1.95
T49620	RICH MAN, POOR MAN	*Irwin Shaw*	£1.60
T51609	MAYDAY	*Thomas H. Block*	£1.75
T54071	MATCHING PAIR	*George G. Gilman*	£1.50
T45773	CLAIRE RAYNER'S LIFEGUIDE		£2.50
T53709	PUBLIC MURDERS	*Bill Granger*	£1.75
T53679	THE PREGNANT WOMAN'S BEAUTY BOOK	*Gloria Natale*	£1.25
T49817	MEMORIES OF ANOTHER DAY	*Harold Robbins*	£1.95
T50807	79 PARK AVENUE	*Harold Robbins*	£1.75
T50149	THE INHERITORS	*Harold Robbins*	£1.75
T53231	THE DARK	*James Herbert*	£1.50
T43245	THE FOG	*James Herbert*	£1.50
T53296	THE RATS	*James Herbert*	£1.50
T45528	THE STAND	*Stephen King*	£1.75
T50874	CARRIE	*Stephen King*	£1.50
T51722	DUNE	*Frank Herbert*	£1.75
T52575	THE MIXED BLESSING	*Helen Van Slyke*	£1.75
T38602	THE APOCALYPSE	*Jeffrey Konvitz*	95p

NEL P.O. BOX 11, FALMOUTH TR10 9EN, CORNWALL

Postage Charge:
U.K. Customers 45p for the first book plus 20p for the second book and 14p for each additional book ordered to a maximum charge of £1.63.

B.F.P.O. & EIRE Customers 45p for the first book plus 20p for the second book and 14p for the next 7 books; thereafter 8p per book.

Overseas Customers 75p for the first book and 21p per copy for each additional book.

Please send cheque or postal order (no currency).

Name ....

Address ....

....

Title ....

While every effort is made to keep prices steady, it is sometimes necessary to increase prices at short notice. New English Library reserve the right to show on covers and charge new retail prices which may differ from those advertised in the text or elsewhere.(7)